T0208022

THE CITY OF PYRAMIDS

SEARCHING FOR THE GOLDEN ALCHEMY

José Manuel Rizzo

BALBOA.PRESS
A DIVISION OF HAY HOUSE

Balboa Press books may be ordered through booksellers or by contacting:

Balboa Press
A Division of Hay House
1663 Liberty Drive
Bloomington, IN 47403
www.balboapress.com
1 (877) 407-4847

Because of the dynamic nature of the Internet, any web addresses or links contained in this book may have changed since publication and may no longer be valid. The views expressed in this work are solely those of the author and do not necessarily reflect the views of the publisher, and the publisher hereby disclaims any responsibility for them.

The author of this book does not dispense medical advice or prescribe the use of any technique as a form of treatment for physical, emotional, or medical problems without the advice of a physician, either directly or indirectly. The intent of the author is only to offer information of a general nature to help you in your quest for emotional and spiritual well-being. In the event you use any of the information in this book for yourself, which is your constitutional right, the author and the publisher assume no responsibility for your actions.

Any people depicted in stock imagery provided by Getty Images are models, and such images are being used for illustrative purposes only. Certain stock imagery © Getty Images.

Edited by Carolina Rizzo and Michael Shelfer

Print information available on the last page.

ISBN: 978-1-9822-3958-9 (sc)
ISBN: 978-1-9822-3959-6 (e)

Balboa Press rev. date: 11/29/2019

DEDICATION

I dedicate this book:

To God for being my guide,

My "Raison d' étre"; my everything.

To Virgin María Auxiliadora (Mary the aid giver) and Little San Juan Bosco (Saint John Bosco) for being my guides and protectors from time immemorial.

To my parents, Lilia and Andrés, who taught me about love, respect and perseverance in my work and goals.

To my true love, Debora, my eternal companion and fundamental pillar in my life. Without her help and support, none of this work would be possible today.

To my Daughter Carolina, an angel sent to me as a gift from heaven, and who came to me to show me the tenderness, love and innocence in the heart of a little girl.

To Raúl Biord, for his unconditional friendship and motivational support to the achievement of my goals.

ACKNOWLEDGEMENTS

Ezequiel has inspired the whole contents of this book. I thank him for his loving will and devotion. I hope all the feeling within him, wide-spreads love throughout the universe, for the understanding of the truths expressed herein. There are those who are in tune with what I have written here.

Others will be so; from the moment they start reading this material. To those who resist accepting these teachings, I send my unconditional love and understanding.

I am convinced that when they receive them, the doors to every possible thing in the universe, will remain opened, for once you get to experience the dimension of peace, you will have found the perfect place to live in.

I am deeply indebted to these great men and women:

My uncle Ambrosio Pérez, and my aunt Miriam Materán. My loving aunt Rita Pérez, who reflects God's light in every smile and whose help, support and unconditional love always stimulated me to search for the true path in my life.

Eduardo and his group for contributing to create Alquimia Dorada's (Golden Alchemy's), "conspiring space", Adriana Felice, whose presence, phone calls, photocopying and organizing efforts, made this marvelous outcome easier. Hiddekel Manriquez, for her cooperation and help to finish this work. Carolina Desiree Rizzo, for reviewing the translation. God bless all of you, and my love to you all.

"The Mandala is a Sacred System, which connects us with the concentric and fleeting energy of the Universe. Its energy lines expand through the four main coordinates: North, South, East, and West. There, in each of them, a sacred portal is born, cared for, and blessed by its Spiritual Protectors."

Dr. José Manuel Rizzo

"A warrior of the Light understands that the Universe is full of mysteries that should be discovered. For this purpose, it is necessary to turn on our Inner Light as a sublime reflection of the Main Energy from the Creator."

Dr. José Manuel Rizzo

"A true warrior of the light knows that this World is full of mysteries, spiritual paths and opportunities, which a Spiritual person can solve and unlock with strength, wisdom and unconditional love. For many reasons, a true warrior of light knows that his Spiritual Power comes from his inner energy in connection with of the sun, rain, wind and the energy of nature."

Dr. José Manuel Rizzo

CONTENTS

Part Five: Internal Chaos

Part Six: Memories from The Future

Part Seven: Global

Part Eight: A Re-Evaluation of The Adventure

Part Nine: The Return Home

PROLOGUE

In the town of little San Juan, there was magic. A magic so ancient, few inhabitants knew about it. Ezequiel was a grandfather in the town with a great secret…he knew about the magic. In this world: where the supernatural is natural. Where one's consciousness can be reawakened as it once was. Where spiritual beings hold the key to the journey of a lifetime. It has been prophesied that there is a girl who can help bring peace and help others gain consciousness. Ezequiel knew of this prophecy and what was to come.

The night Ezequiel left was like any other night. His granddaughter, Jazmin, sat at the kitchen table writing while his daughter cooked in the kitchen. Ezequiel was meditating, trying to connect with his spiritual beings to receive answers about a feeling he had. He travelled to a meadow filled with white flowers and surrounded by trees. Two bright, glowing beings emitting yellow light stood at the middle of it, their palms extended, as if to welcome him. "Ezequiel," they said, their voices warm and welcoming, "Welcome."

"Hello, who are you?", Ezequiel asked.

"We are the guardians of the meadow. Our names are not important, but our message is," they said, their voices echoing across the meadow.

"What message?"

"We have the answers which you seek Ezequiel."

Ezequiel nodded, moving from the edge of the treeline and walking closer to them until he stood right in front of them.

"What is the message?"

"It is time for you to travel to where change is necessary. It is prophesised that once you leave, a great time will pass before the change will begin, but your absence is the key to the change."

"Where is this change?"

"You will find out along the way. You must trust in your spiritual beings and in yourself."

Ezequiel nodded in understanding, then a worried look fell across his face.

"My family?"

"They will be okay, we promise we will watch over them."

Ezequiel smiled, "When shall I leave?"

"The sooner the better. The journey is long, and on this journey, you will experience a great change."

"I am ready for all things. I feel ready."

"You are," they answered, their voices ringing in unison.

He suddenly saw three glittering lights enter the meadow. They swirled behind the two beings until they began to glow and slowly became human-like figures.

"They will join you on your journey. They will help you get to where you need to go."

The three beings walked closer to him their respective purple, green, and blue light-like bodies glowing. They got behind him, two on each side and one behind him, encasing him in a light filled cocoon. Suddenly, the trees parted in the middle, revealing a rocky path. The two beings passed, leaving the path open for Ezequiel to walk through. With the three beings surrounding him, he walked forward toward the path. He stopped pausing to look at the two other beings. "Thank you," he said. He felt a sense of happiness, excitement, and honour about the task at hand.

He walked onto the path and continued onward. The more he walked, the more he felt himself returning to his body. Slowly, the vision faded and he opened his eyes. His granddaughter stood in front of him, smiling.

"Grandpa, I'm going to bed."

He smiled and hugged her, "Goodnight Jazmin, I love you."

"I love you too grandpa. Goodnight, see you tomorrow."

Ezequiel's smile didn't dim, although he realized she would not see him tomorrow.

"Goodnight dad," his daughter said, "See you tomorrow."

"Goodnight."

As his family went toward their rooms, he slowly slipped out the door to begin the first step to the great adventure.

- Written by Carolina D. Rizzo

INTRODUCTION

The first Kings and Emperors of the universe had a set of codes through which they ruled. These codes were based on ancient principles of benevolent rule, inherited from lost kingdoms such as Atlantis, Lemuria, and The Mayan Empire. These principles were taught to the people throughout the kingdom so that they would follow those basic rules. A Mandala integrated these principles or passwords (nine for this dimension), which were interpreted in different ways and have the capabilities to remove inhibitions, change attitudes, and keep connected all the planes in The Universe.

It is of vital importance to find The Sacred Password in order to defeat all the obstacles that block the way to the spiritual world and rescue that jewel which makes any human wish come true in this dimension. The right interpretation of the Mandala opens up a secret and sacred dimensional portal. This portal has been guarded under maximum security for many centuries. From a subtle plane, Ezequiel has followed the path to this portal that leads the way into a world of diamond-like reality, where all healing and wisdom coexist. This is the center that activates the vital energy of The Universe and allows communication with The Kingdom of God Most High.

The discovery of the password is always associated to a vow or promise that must be honored through eternity, under the penalty that your intentions and wishes never be granted. Ezequiel knows the four guardsmen who watch the access to the temple; their mission is to guide those chosen to The City of Pyramids, to the discovery of The Sacred Password.

PART ONE

AWAKENINGS AND VISIONS

EZEQUIEL'S DISAPPEARANCE

The inhabitants of Little San Juan shared the thought that the woods kept strange surprises and mysteries. Twenty-six years had passed by since the last time Ezequiel would tell Jazmin, his seven-year-old granddaughter, old traditional stories dating more than half a century. It hadn't seemed like such a long time since Jazmin last visited her grandfather's cabin. Ezequiel was missing now, and the police had stopped the search because the possibilities of him being alive were very scarce from the standpoint of the police. Ezequiel had gone deeply into the woods, beyond the threshold of reality, into a place where hundreds of people arrived with no return ticket, searching for the great secret: the mythical password to access The City of Pyramids.

Jazmin felt too much at ease, given the unfortunate events around her. She kept silent and listened very carefully to everything the neighbors and the police had to tell her before going into the home where she shared so many of her dreams with her grandfather during her childhood.

Built on the hilltop, the house had a panoramic view of the town. The humming of a fresh serpent-like creek could be heard in the midst of the old trees that, at several meters high, would be telling three-hundred-year-old stories. Curiously enough, Little San Juan was the town chosen by mystics coming to the world from even the most remote places of the planet to a new spiritual awakening, where everyone lets themselves be carried away by fate. One day, Ezequiel started up the fateful walk towards the threshold of time, to get into the scenery now deployed before Jazmin's own eyes. She was thinking about Ezequiel.

My grandpa is a wise man, she assured herself. *He always says that God created little San Juan. This town has a secret portal that leads to man's true essence.*

While taking a stroll into the woods, her mind was busy with images from her childhood. Things that even now, she couldn't understand; but one thing she was sure about: her grandpa Ezequiel, was a really wise man. After twenty-six years, that conviction was still intact.

When Jazmin was a little girl, she would cheerfully go look for Old Ezequiel sometimes because she believed she saw sparks of light. Once her friends got there to see them, the sparks would have mysteriously disappeared. As time passed, she thought that her mind was playing tricks on her because none of her friends ever saw the sparks. From then on, the lights made themselves very scarce until one day, they were gone altogether. Now, Jazmin was busy with things that a girl from the city does.

She missed being with her grandparents in Little San Juan, where at every sunset, her grandpa Ezequiel invited her to see the sacred energy field emanating from all town inhabitants, which according to him, could be seen from the house-porch. All the while, she would make unsuccessful efforts to see it, but it wouldn't work. To her, it felt nice just being there, sitting beside her grandpa, keeping him company, and looking out on such a wonderful landscape.

Today, right at six p.m., everyone in Little San Juan was focused on one thought, as customary: to speed up the rhythm of chance in their lives and to flow with the people's collective wisdom. That day, the combined intention was centered so strongly in Ezequiel's reappearance that it could have moved a huge mountain.

Jazmin walked to the edge of the woods, wanting to find out what the sparks were made up of. Occasionally, she would see them at night, and often she asked herself whether they were only seen in Little San Juan.

Grandpa said that the sparks were men transformed into energy. They lived to keep this dimension connected to a higher one, where The City of Pyramids exists. Every single night, Ezequiel would say to the girl: "Be calm and sleep peacefully, because the rebirth of Little San Juan is slowly becoming," and she would fall asleep imagining how that could be, while holding onto that thought. She was convinced, deep down in her heart, that if she were to follow the sparks of light, she'd eventually enter the dimension her grandfather dwells in now, perhaps transformed into energy: the kind of energy she'd seen as sparks of light.

That's how this story starts, and Jazmin recounted:

"I remember when I was a little girl, I would climb up the enormous branches of a huge tree, way down my house. The tree was the only one amid a clean piece of land in between the house and the woods ahead. It was three times taller than me with a very strong and thick trunk. Everyone used to call that place, 'the cove,' although it had no resemblance to a cove, but the name sounded interesting and inviting to adventure and mystery," said Jazmin.

"The cove holds a kind of magic because it has miraculously survived the progress of asphalt, buildings, and plastic. My child-like sensitivity was pleased to find out that 'the cove' was still standing there and just so maybe the lights too.

"There was a field beside grandpa's house where some twenty horses used to graze. Ezequiel would say that unicorns would come in the middle of the night; he had seen them. I'm sure of it, because grandpa would never tell a lie. But things change, and now there are about eighty houses built, and about fifty more being built on what used to be only grass, flowers, and butterflies. Little San Juan's new inhabitants are very grateful for these shelters. Grandpa would always say that the one man that would change the world had been born in Little San Juan.

"I've come to meet him and I'm sure grandpa is with him right now. The man that will change the world comes from The City of Pyramids. One day, he flew up to the sky and transformed into a being of pure light, but not before promising he'd be back."

PART TWO

IMAGES AT THE THRESHOLD OF REALITY

THE RETURN OF THE MAN LIVING IN LITTLE SAN JUAN'S WOODS

The woods were filled with mystics. In the past twenty-six years, I have visited a good many place, found exceptional beings in different endeavors, at different churches and universities, but none like Mr. Way, a tall man of white complexion, black hair, and blue eyes, who would walk through the woods, carrying a leather bag filled with crystal-like precious stones.

He's a weird guy, he has his eccentricities. He always lived in the woods of Little San Juan. Sometimes he'd be out of everyone's eyesight for long periods of time and people would ask:

"What has become of Mr. Way? Could the old man be dead?"

But whenever least expected, he'd show up once again at the town's bar, smoking his strange pipe.

Mr. Way lived in a hidden cabin, deep in the woods right in the middle of several centenary trees. The cabin was so concealed, sometimes it seemed as if the earth had swallowed it, as if it had suddenly vanished. He said that each one of those trees is a wise master who has all the wisdom in the universe inside them. We had to ask the wise trees where the cabin is.

Grandpa Ezequiel said that Mr. Way has the capabilities to connect with the sacred-energy field. Mr. Way often said that Jazmin means humbleness, the most important condition to travel successfully through time. I always felt the potential within to be able to do so, because I am Jazmin, and when I reconnected with the giant trees and the cove, I realized why I had returned home. I felt very much moved and with a sense of having to follow my hunches.

I knew grandpa had found The Sacred Password and was now traveling in the dimension of the light sparks heading to The City of Pyramids. I just wanted to join his journey.

Actually, there was something, or someone, who was taking me somewhere within myself; to that place where I could find the password, that key of sacred connection; or maybe I was just nearing a great discovery. But from then on, I started to experience a brilliant image with sparks of light, just like the ones I'd known when I was a girl. At first, I felt the fear of the unknown, but I so very much wished to run into Mr. Way that I forgot the feeling altogether, knowing that he could clear up the mystery.

The cool breeze was blowing my hair around. I shut my eyes and grandpa's wise words came to mind: "If you can dream of it, you can certainly do it." I opened my eyes and thought I was in the middle of dream. There he was, Mr. Way; standing about thirty-two feet away from where I was. Curiously enough, he hadn't changed one bit in the twenty-six years I hadn't seen him. Mr. Way happily smiled at me and said:

"I'm so glad you're here! I was waiting for you." Mr. Way was wearing a pair of blue pants, a flannel shirt with squares on it, and a pair of boots. I guessed him to be about fifty years old. He smelled like fresh grass. He looked so white as if just having taken a shower. I wanted to ask him how he knew I'd be here, for him to be waiting for me so assuredly, but I was so startled I could barely tell him:

"Something in my heart tells me you can help me." He nodded his head, and the way he stared at me left me speechless. Silently, we looked at each other and in a somewhat weird way; I understood that we were remembering each other from another time and place. It was a strange vision, where once again, the sparks of light were present, only this time they were bigger, shinier, and stayed for a longer period of time.

Grandpa used to say that Mr. Way could read people's thoughts as well as the intentions of men's hearts; that is why he is the caretaker of Little San Juan's woods.

"We need to talk," Mr. Way told me.

I asked, "How did you . . .?" He didn't even let me finish the question.

"It was just an assumption on my part," he interrupted. "Many people come to the woods to appreciate its beauty. Others come to find themselves and others, or to restart on their mission's path."

"I know the man who is going to change the world is in Little San Juan and I want to meet him. Where is my grandfather?", I asked, and he turned east towards the sun.

"In the middle of the woods, it is possible to find him sometimes. It's a matter of luck."

"A matter of luck? What do you mean by that?"

"It is when preparation and opportunity coincide. Only those who get to unlock the mysteries along the path can find the key to awaken the magic to transform their visions. Very few souls have found the password. A few beings, like your grandfather, arrived at the threshold of reality and have undertaken the adventure of unravel the mystery. It is a captivating quest with the purpose of reaching the highest level of consciousness on earth, which dwells right here in Little San Juan's woods."

"Is grandpa in any kind of danger?"

"Well, there could be a remote possibility, and the answer lies in his choice of thoughts. If he chooses to think he is in danger, he will create the conditions for dangerous situations to occur. Everything is arranged to materialize anything set in your heart and mind. The universe executes the will of men. That is the lesson."

"Could I meet him? Will I be able to discover the password and enter The City of Pyramids?"

"Calm down! Take a deep breath and let the answer flow from your heart."

"How will I know that I received the answer?", I asked.

"Because I have created myself with that sacred energy, just like my Egyptian, Lemurian, Atlantean and Mayan ancestors did for thousands of years. That's the one place in the world that holds all the medicine, wisdom, gifts, and paths humans experience thoroughly in the adventure of living. This place keeps and holds the essence of Genesis, of everything that has been, is, and will be."

"Do you still want to meet the man that will change the world?"

"Of course! . . . When do we leave?", Jazmin hurriedly said.

"We are already on our way. The invincible force of attraction of the ascendant is the appropriate vehicle at this moment, and your decision is the fuel this vehicle uses. We are entering into the heart of the woods, it is best to be trustful and let ourselves go."

A very strong desire to make new discoveries alternated with images of fear of the unknown in my mind. Curiously, seconds later, every one of those frightening images would appear before me. I'd see huge terrifying dragons stalking me and also beautiful, luminescent fairies flying around everywhere. Mr. Way observed me attentively, and I could appreciate a strange mixture of pleasure and compassion in his stare.

"Just relax," he said. "Breathe and let go. All of that is in your mind. It is safe and easy to follow the impulse of your heart. It is the only way to go higher; the demons you see only show up when you try to stop the journey. Close your eyes so you can see the brilliance of your vital inner star and focus yourself on its endless flow. At times, you'll see a light like that of a sunset, getting dimmer and dimmer like the end of any day. The truth is that simultaneously, the rebirth of the light is taking place in another place, further away to the east. Your mission is to keep yourself fixed on its brilliance, because that light lights up your way, and if you are not careful enough, you could end up in darkness, experiencing over and over again the constant misfortunes of trial and error."

I shut my eyes closed and let myself go in between rhythmical sighs to an unknown destination towards the light, where time doesn't exist.

PART THREE

UNICORNS

THE FIRST UTOPIA

For a few moments, Jazmin ran out of thoughts. She felt paralyzed as the last sunrays were coloring the shadowy skies orange. Mr. Way was with her; he never left her side. Suddenly, the thundering sound of galloping horses was heard from some unknown place in the woods; it seemed like hundreds of horses. Out of fear, Jazmin was breathing very heavily. Darkness had enveloped them with its thick cloak, as if to announce that mysterious things were about to happen.

"What is happening? Are we in danger?", I asked, gasping.

"Ask your heart. Breathe in and let yourself listen to the voice of your heart," said Mr. Way. He had just seen Crosstemps approaching them. His intense, big blue eyes, staring deeply, looked like two gleaming crystals in the dark. He was the leader of the herd of unicorns that was getting closer and closer. Jazmin knew about unicorns because of the marvelous stories her grandfather would tell her many times before she was sent away to the city to grow up and study. She was about to become a law-graduate and couldn't believe her eyes, for what she was seeing right at that moment was creating an inner conflict. She was now certain that unicorns did exist. Jazmin looked in complete awe at Crosstemps, as he was shining under the moonlight nearing her in the darkness. Then, before she could catch her breath, Crosstemps spoke:

"I greet the omniscient wisdom that blesses your souls with unconditional love from the very essence of the Divine Mother and the Divine Father."

"Hi Crosstemps. How are you, my good friend?", Mr. Way said happily.

"I'm always good," replied Crosstemps.

"Strength, faith, and spirituality!", I hurriedly whispered, astonished and motivated; my grandpa Ezequiel would always say that the sight of a unicorn would always bring the magic of strength, faith, and spirituality with it.

"That is so!", said Crosstemps. "Your faith has given you the strength to be here now and to discover from spirituality, a conscious path towards The Light. I offer you my wings to take you beyond The East, where you will find the password to enter The City of Pyramids."

"Will I find my grandpa?"

"All your wishes are accepted, expressed, and realized. In order to attain this, you must rid yourself of every obstacle in your way and wake up in the New Little San before dawn, and before the sun of perfect love comes out."

"How can I achieve this?"

"Unfolding your true feelings and wishes so that the fountain of sacred energy within you radiates wisdom and benevolence."

"Mr. Way, are you telling me that here, I'm going to find all the fantastic beings in grandpa's bedtime stories? What kind of fantasy is this? Am I dreaming?", I asked.

"Dear Jazmin, all of our feelings come from two main sources: love and fear. Human nature is love, and fear is a force created to seize the world. It has never been real, however it has developed the ability to show itself very large, so much so, that love hides itself, waiting for the right moment in which everyone finds enough courage to know the truth. A very long time ago, everyone had access to the password and The Golden Alchemy was a common good; but King Cicero took it away, and ever since, has kept it hidden during several centuries, waiting for the man who will change the world. The King thinks that he can somehow negotiate The Golden Alchemy with the man that will change the world, and together, rule from the center of The World. You must go into The Kingdom of The City of Pyramids and defeat **Midas**, a rebel who will try to hurt you, but only when you are in complete harmony with The Light will you be able to annihilate him, since he is just an illusion. He is in your mind and in the mind of every human being. From there, he exists as an illusion, an illusion you create and let be. Evil is nonexistent. You are my beloved Jazmin and your mission is to go to the world and tell the truth."

"What truth are you talking about? I just want to find my grandfather, discover The Sacred Password, and go to The City of Pyramids to meet the man that will change the world."

"Right now, your grandfather is within parallel planes of existence, just like you are now; there is a future, a present, and a past. The ways of life are vertical containers of events, activated by the outflow of electrifying impulses from our thoughts and feelings. At times, we call it luck, but it is really life's main creating mechanism, a collective gift that lives in the soul of the world."

"Jazmin, close your eyes and breathe slowly with a steady rhythm. Let the images of love flow through your conscious mind now," Mr. Way said. Jazmin closed her eyes and breathed slowly and rhythmically; little by little, she fell into a state of special relaxation. The Images, her memories, were passing by, without her stopping on any particular one, like watching clouds go by. Dominique, the loyal German Shepherd she used to play with when she was a little kid, was the first image that impacted her, and there she stopped for a while. It was an authentic projection; but was it really Dominique?

He got sick one night and grandpa would give him several teaspoons of some miraculous waters to make him feel better. He said: "What is happening is that it is time for Dominique to learn new things; that's why he is growing wings. Dominique, as well as you and me, he is made up of the same essence and he can never die, but if he chooses to leave now, that's all right; he'll come back when once again he chooses the reality of love. Dominique is invincible because this is magic, and we'll find each other again."

The memory of her dog touched her so deeply that she opened her eyes. Jazmin heard something moving behind her, under the tenuous moonlight; she watched herself. and the surprise paralyzed her respiration for an instant. Something was flying towards her and once it got closer, she shivered at the sight of Dominique. Before she could decide, the flying dog had landed at a clearing in the woods where she was. It occurred to her that it was an impossible idea, although, during all her childhood years, she wanted nothing more in the world then to confirm what her grandpa said. Dominique had grown wings. Mr. Way and Crosstemps, the Unicorn, seemed to be the only witnesses of such an experience at the threshold of reality. A beautiful light was flowing out of Dominique's funny body.

"Is that really you, Dominique? Where were you?", Jazmin asked.

"In your heart," the flying dog happily affirmed. "What do you think about my new abilities? Now I can fly and speak your own language! Where are your good manners?"

"I'm sorry Dominique; it's just that I feel so…"

"Oh, yes! I know; German Shepherds aren't supposed to talk, but only understand, right? Well, now you know that all dogs have magic, although our manners may not be all that refined," he lamented. Jazmin remembered what she dreamt of the days after Dominique's disappearance; those dreams had been so real.

People appeared who she had seen somewhere. She concentrated a lot, trying to remember who they were. She covered her face and pressed her eyes to make sure that she was sleeping and that everything was a dream. Then, she removed her hands from her face, and it was clear to her that Dominique was really there; she had seen him fly and his body was surrounded by light. The dream was definitely real, and Dominique was magic and light, reminding her of that old universal aphorism: if you can dream of it, it will certainly come true.

PART FOUR

RECALLING WISDOM

THE TREE OF JUSTICE

Little San Juan's woods had the appearance exactly like that of the respectable woods in a fairy tales. Once again, Mr. Way seemed to guess my thoughts and remarked:

"Each one of these trees represents, in itself, each one of the spiritual foundations of humans: Justice, Truth, Common Good, Unconditional Love, Integrity, Intuition, Forgiveness, Compassion, and Gratitude. If you were to embrace every one of them, you would be able to feel life's pulse, listen to the rumor of times, nurture yourself, and balance your roots. They are the strength that will let you overcome all the great trials you have to go through to discover the password that will take you into the City of Pyramids."

"How will I know which trees are the right ones? There are hundreds of them in the woods and they all look alike."

"Ask your heart, just breathe deeply, and listen to the voice of your heart. Close your eyes and let your heart pick, for your heart is wise and has no limits, but your thought is intelligent and finite," Mr. Way said.

Jazmin felt the foolishness of her own behavior. Great things had already happened in the woods with plenty of demonstrations: first, Crosstemps, a unicorn, which supposedly does not exist, then Dominique, a luminescent, flying dog that can talk, and on top of all that, Mr. Way's sparkles that seemed to get bigger and shinier, getting closer and closer all the time; it had to be a dream!

"Well, what does it matter? If I am really asleep, I better keep my eyes shut."

She closed her eyes and let herself be guided by the elementals, like cosmic music letting her vibrant body be taken into the light. It was nature's own rhythm at work, like angels singing unedited harmonies of voices and instruments in a celestial choir. She was totally awake and conscious, with her heart set on all her senses. She turned her attention into the middle of her heart, knowing that everything would be all right, and surrendered herself to an embrace without time, the Tree of Justice, to experiment with nature's rhythm.

A part of Jazmin would have wanted to ask: *and what now?* But something inside made her feel it was not such a good idea to doubt faith right that moment. An almost imperceptible spasm could be seen going across Jazmin's white countenance and her entire body broke out goosebumps while she surrendered herself to the experience. Behind the strange expression on her face, there was a very intense battle going on between the most basic instincts of the young student. The young student had to decide whether to go on, and happily let herself march toward adventure in an eternal dimension, experimenting the warmth of the energy waves that made her vibrate from head to toes. Or, on the other hand, dismiss the experience all together and return to her, looking for a logical, scientific explanation with high probabilities of having her law-school-friends' approval.

Mr. Way realized what was happening inside her. He had a very peculiar glare in his eyes, and softly, he said:

"It's quite all right to trust life's process. Breathe and open yourself up to receive no matter where it comes from or who sends it. It is your heart's miracle; everyone has his or her own way to learn the lessons from both worlds. Each person has an access key and a way to get across time and space. Trust the power within you to learn from yourself, that's the only way you'll get all you need to get to The City of Pyramids and find the password. This is the time to fight; accept it. It is all right to let a helping hand guide us, encouraged by The Great Lord of The Woods."

But Jazmin had no intentions of letting go of the experience she had already passed beyond the threshold of anything credible, and she was ready to accept every new lesson. She wouldn't miss discovering the password and meeting with her grandfather once again. So, she relaxed, took a deep breath, and enjoyed the contact with The Tree of Justice.

She could almost see the inner engagements of justice under the wise old sage's thick tree-bark. Once more, she saw the sparks of light. Once again, the sparks and the intense luminescence was in front of her, bigger, brighter, and more permanent each time. Beside the tree, there was a beautiful white angora cat called Urano and an elegant steed called Max. The first one was The Master of Cleverness, Intelligence, Wit, and Happiness. The horse knew every angle of nobleness and the power of good intentions. Max and Urano joined Mr. Way, teaming up with Dominique and Crosstemps. The team's mission was to escort Jazmin all the way through this adventurous quest to meet King Cicero, Ruler of The City of Pyramids.

It is peculiarly interesting to see how all of the trees in Little San Juan are free to express what they want and be understood by the men in these woods. Jazmin couldn't help but be surprised when bright sparks in the shape of a whirlwind came out of the wood's Giant and swirled around her trembling body. For an instant, she thought of running away to hide because she didn't understand what was going on; but then, she heard The Tree of Justice Say:

"From the eternal Atlantis, I bring here old lessons humanity needs to remember. The first one of them is ethics; that is, acting under moral principles. Ethics is the straightness every human being identifies inside themselves and every single moment of his or her life. Being ethical is a way of life, a behavior; it is feeling good about what it is being done, what you think, and what you accomplish," explained the millenary tree, its leafy branches now looking protective.

"That's true," added Dominique while flying in circles with the birds announcing dawn. "Humans need to reprogram ethical values, beginning with justice, understood as giving everybody what they deserve. It involves giving each and every one of the living creatures of this living planet which vibrates intensely with our actions."

Jazmin reflected about love and how, in spite of all the writings and discussions about it, many thinkers still look for the true meaning of love. It seems that to love and to live are lessons difficult to learn from books alone. The ancient tree, as well as Mr. Way, seemed to read her thoughts and replied:

"To love is to feel life as something proper of the creator. It is feeling that every action, thought, and your own intelligence obeys, and at the same time, is the creation of that sublime, dynamic and intelligent energy within all that exists, and which rules over everything. That is the wonderful energy, which inspired your grandparents and gave them the required courage to get across the threshold of reality and see things through a different viewpoint. This is unconditional love, and it too has its own ethics."

"The ethics of unconditional love! How did you come up with that?", asked the surprised girl.

"From the universe where the ethics of unconditional love dwell. It is an energy system integrated by nine parts engaged to each other. Do you really wish to know about them?"

"But of course, I'd love to."

"To know them puts you in a compromising situation of vital commitment, for once you know this truth, you've already started to walk on a path of no return. Once you've seen the light, it will be difficult to return to the world of shadows."

"Fine, I am ready." Jazmin said.

"The first one corresponds to the **Authenticity of Being**. That means that your acts and thoughts must be oriented to the progressive development of man. Work is the means to realize that giving to someone else out of sincerity, affection, and truth is the most powerful tool to create a way of living, being, and feeling where individuals related to their kindred can feel, live, and are happy with the reality around them," so explained The Tree of Justice.

"Well, yes…", interrupted Jazmin, very much interested. "But would you please, tell me some more about the authenticity of being?"

"Sure; an authentic being is he who connects himself to his true self; when he looks at himself in the mirror, he is looking into the mirror of the soul and really appreciates his flaws and virtues. He says to himself: I love you. He offers to the universe and others his inner truth and recognizes that under the protection of positive energy, everything heals and is made possible. He knows that reality is just a partial vision around man, for when he looks at it as a whole, he understands that his aptitude and attitude, from an ethical standpoint, make him grand, honest, and permeable to all of life's circumstances, which lead to ends of material and spiritual prosperity."

"That sounds interesting; it is similar to a conference a professor once gave at my University; but how can man show himself as being authentic?"

"Well, he has to work with one of his most important gifts: the rightful use of his free will, and always **being firm with whatever he chooses do decide**; that's the second part of it. Deciding something is always a good choice, because when you do, you put to work a God-given divine thought at its very essence. This is the energy of fairness; it is the connection of the self from being to being to make individual or collective goals come true. Doubt is a sin of those who never do anything and are always complaining about something. Doubt and complaint are contrary to love, for firmness integrates strength of character, sincerity, and humbleness into any decision you make. Firmness is to set aside the comfort of what you know, to venture into unexplored ground to come up with a sincere word, a kind treatment to others and a true thought. Firmness lets you know who you really are, what you came here for, and where you are supposed to go."

"And where am I going?", asked Jazmin, a bit confused. "You mean, where are we all going, right?", interrupted Dominique, while Crosstemps, Urano, and Max nodded their heads with the intention to journey along with her in her mission.

"Of course, you are all going to your own **Reconciliation with life**," said the Tree of Justice. "And that's the third part of it. Your job is to fully understand that life is an inexhaustible fountain of experiences. Life is like water: fresh, sweet, crystal-clear, pure, and vital. It is to know and to feel that we are a part of it and that our destiny is in our hands here and now. To reconcile with life is to appreciate the beauty of a country and its people. Also, it is to know how to confront situations and things that are not so pleasant to us; overcome what we are able to overcome. Love what we think is not possible to love; understand that the noblest of things in a human being is inner love, as well as being totally convinced that the best thing you've learned since the very first days of your existence is to love."

"How do you love? I feel people are confused about it." Immediately, the Tree of Justice was filled with a sweet aroma that spread to the woods all around us.

"Love is the vision we get when we are in someone else's shoes. It is to feel what the other feels, suffer what the other suffers, and be happy when someone else is happy. It is to be in tune with everyone and everything. It is to be conscious of yourself being a part of a solar system and a galaxy that is never alone by itself. It is to reconcile with your spiritual self. It is to feel in the innermost part of your soul that you are valuable and that the creator loves you, respects you and admires you. It is to look at yourself in the mirror and be able to say: I love you, I respect you, and I admire you."

"I believe that even though I don't say those things to myself very often, I do appreciate myself," assured Jazmin.

"Well, but maybe you require **to be a more unconditional self; that is the fourth step.** It's like going into the woods and falling under the impression that you'll never be able to leave from there. Some of your loved ones will stay out of the woods and you will not be able to see them, talk to them, or feel them; on top of all that, you will only see the initial part of the woods, not all of it. And you'll have to thoroughly explore it in order to see the truth it hides. The self is, and will always be, the enigma of the world. In order to find it, you first have to look for it. To look for it, you first have to feel it. To feel it, you have to see it. And to see it, you have to visualize it. That implies developing a **Capacity to feel, love, and live**; that's the fifth step."

"What does Justice have to do with the capacity to feel, to love, and to live? Then, what is justice?"

"They are related from the whole to the parts; in other words, there is justice if you feel the tenderness, warmth, and humbleness of a child. But there is also justice if you love your spouse, children, relatives, and all the humble people. Justice is living humbly, practicing the workings of the heart, making no distinctions between classes, race, or religion. It is living as if it is your last day, doing what is good and avoiding doing what is bad. It is transforming hate, revenge, resentment, lies, and negative thoughts in our lives. Justice is a value that you can find with the ethical practice of acting in the behavior of love in your family and in society, where integrity and compassion dissipate and transform everything."

"Are you talking to me about forgiveness?"

"Yes of course . . . It is forgiving, to attain happiness. Happiness being a state of consciousness where everything takes you to the knowledge of the self through everything and the one. For one is all and all is one, given that the essence of a person is the one, just as everybody's essence is the one. Man's happiness lies in living life satisfied with every one of his own body cells, knowing he can breathe; being able to appreciate a living person's caress; that is, being satisfied with the tiniest and the largest things in existence. It is also to commit oneself to one's mission, one's existence, one's essence, which is the same as the essence of the creator. It is to unite oneself with wisdom, consciousness, pleasure, love, rejoice, passion, creation to live the truth of life's energy, intelligent energy, forgiveness, and unconditional love. The essence is life.

"That is what I call living!", Urano said and sighed.

"It is life itself!", concluded Max.

"That is so," the Tree of Justice kept on talking. "Because **Life itself** is the sixth step. Life is the soul's mirror. It starts up its own existence, making it fly off its own way. An eagle flies because it wants to, and a man flies if he wants to. A man lives if he wants to; an eagle lives because it wants to. A man loves if he wants to love; an eagle loves because it wants to love. A man feels if he wants to feel. An eagle feels because it wants to feel. And the eagle loves because God wants it to love, and man loves because God wants him to love. God wants what man wants; wanting is the creating instrument of God's word. Because God wants what man wants, because when he wants, he wants to create what he wants and live what he wants and how he wants."

"You confuse me in the way you explain things…but I gather you mean… Justice is the same as Unconditional love?"

"Bingo, You're right once again. **Unconditional Love is Justice.**"

Jazmin's more rebellious self asked: "Why is it that no one can see or touch Justice? Why can't you smell it or feel it? Why can't it be loved? Why does it seem that in so many situations and places in the world. . .it does not exist?"

She didn't have to wait long for the answer: "It is because that is not real justice. True Justice is recognized because when felt, I feel it; when seen, I see it; when touched, I touch it; and when loved, I love it. It is feeling deep within one's core every one of life's actions. It is thinking correctly without feeling that one is being harassed to do it. It is giving and receiving life itself, with integrity, wisdom, and humbleness. It is to know man from man and not for man. It is to merge into an endless embrace of doing, feeling, and acting correctly, giving everyone what they deserve without prejudice, taboos, or limitations."

"Innocence is required. . .as you know like a child," Jazmin added. "That's difficult these days."

"On the contrary, we all have it through our pure consciousness, the sublime truth of knowing that everything is one, and that one is everything. Relating to the planet cannot be enrichment without first a just cause to nature; but obtaining those resources is circumscribed to a receiving of that living being that surrounds us and shelters us with tenderness. . .The Planet. This is the basis to build new laws and new ways to interrelate to society."

"Are you talking of a new order and a real change in the administration of justice based on innocence?"

"Perhaps in the innocence and peace, because justice, like life, will always have two poles."

"It depends on each one of us to find a true and fair equilibrium. Now is the moment and opportunity for the structures of justice to change, through love, divine intelligence, and the elevated creative essence. The time has come for us to recognize that the current structures of justice do not correspond to this concept. There can't be justice without peace, fairness, brotherhood, and a physical or legal order of things, which could guarantee the stability, preservation and conservation of the planet, as well as in regard to the correct rules to interpret, exercise and protect Man's Essential Rights."

"That sounds utopian," said Jazmin to gift importance to the Tree of Justice's reflection.

"Now is the time of those who dedicate their lives to the "impossible." One of them has to do with conscious Legislation. This is where laws are not an imposition but are in tune with human beings through their beliefs, which they know through their natural reason in an unequivocal way. This is the time to create an awareness of justice and fairness in human beings. Man must no longer look at the world from an angle that only serves him particularly in a selfish, superficial way. He needs to wake up from the long-lived lethargy to find once more the humane, sensitive, humble conception of justice.

"Justice is a common benefit to all thinking and non-thinking creatures dwelling in this universe. For without the materialization of this concept, life would not exist in terms of real life. Love is life, life is truth, and truth is and will always be fair, now and forever, in the way that truth and justice are the inevitable basis for life. Live life with truthfulness and justice and you will triumph. Jesus Christ once said: 'truth will set you free.' And today I say to you that truth and justice, through love, will make you change your ways towards the father and towards the most elevated, profound, and recondite place of your inner self, for self is nothing more than a part of everything and the one.

"God has given man the possibility to act fairly or unfairly. If he acts fairly, he will be acting from his inner-being; but on the contrary, if he acts unjustly, he will be doing it from his ego. The two tools that man possess to be on the right way and live in righteousness are truth and love. As long as his actions come from there, the result will be fair. If he acts from a contaminated ego, the result will be envy, resentment, revenge, death, and destruction. The contamination of the ego can be destroyed with knowledge of the inner-being, which really comes down to recognition of God's love within us."

"How does God see Justice?"

"Justice seen from God's viewpoint; it is easy to draw a landscape on a canvas, or to record a beautiful sunset with a video camera. But it is very difficult to picture in our minds what is fair to God and what his vision is on this matter; many people throughout life question God for war, famine in the world, or lack of understanding. Some even dare to demand and impose on God. 'God, create Justice, lower your vengeful hand,' but as a result, it would be very easy for God to do it. Only with a thousandth of movements with the blink of his eyes could he reach it."

"But, would that be Justice?", asked Jazmin.

"It would be an imposed Justice, where essential recognition of the human being would be missing. God's Justice is the kind of Justice that lets man make mistakes and learn his lesson from pain or joy. That means that when you see that something unfair is going on, think what your part is, what responsibility do I have with the rest of the human beings in this, and what will I have to do for the correct thing to happen?"

"Then, is Justice a Divine Order? Does God's Justice imply a Divine Order that orders men on the planet's surface? Does this mean that if someone acts in an incorrect way, this special Devine Order will impose itself so that individuals can reflect and change? Many of today's scientists are studying and researching climate changes that are being produced.

They haven't even thought to themselves, could it have anything to do with God's Justice?"

"This is about the energy of love, created by God, which is putting things back in their natural balance and harmonious order. God's Justice is a Divine Essential plan; it is to build organized societies projected from what is essential of human beings and not from political organizations acting as intermediaries, so that individuals are once again what is most important and not the state. Because the rulers of the world only crave to remain in power, or how to overcome the polls and how to maintain control over the citizens they govern. For those reasons, violence is seen in villages, given that these structures are bad from the beginning, because they are vertical. That means there is always one person that imposes his ideas and the rest just execute them. It is impossible to find God's Justice in such a structure, because God's justice is not in the state, but in all citizens networking their way to common goals. Where the state is a horizontal structure and not a vertical one, where a maid and a governor's opinions can both be validated in the decision-making process."

"But that is impossible? That is a utopia?"

"Well, maybe there is a need for more people to dedicate themselves to the impossible. It is neither impossible nor utopia; perhaps, this is not the conventional answer everyone might expect. It is neither wild capitalism, nor neo-liberalism; it is not communism, and it is not Marxism. It is not traditional democracy as we know it, and it is not a dictatorship; instead it is an answer that must be understood from your heart and which later penetrates your reasoning, and just then and only then will you be able to fully understand and create the consciousness of justice that we require."

"What is the simple way to reach Justice?"

"Be happy with what you have: happiness is reachable only if you want to reach it. At times we may think that happiness is money, sexual pleasure, and the compulsive accumulation of material things more and more all the time, but true happiness is only found in the self, understood as a being of endless talents, gifts, and abilities."

"What does happiness have to do with Justice?"

"It has everything to do with it. If there is justice, there is prosperity; if there is justice there is love and with justice you have work, because Justice is a perfect order and its aim is to give man, spirit, live-beings, and universe a full understanding of what it is and how it works, harmonizing every known material aspect and those not yet known. Justice is considered a natural reason and is always there, somewhat stagnant, but ever present. For example, it is like a boy waiting to ride his bike without the wheels or handle. Humans pretend to be happy, without a true knowledge of self and without being conscious of the great truth: you should always do good and offer good things onto others, because when we act the right way, we make ourselves better-thinking, intelligent beings. Happiness is a sacred channel justice expresses itself through. That's the reason human beings are not happy. They want to be happy doing unfair acts, thinking the wrong way and feeling that money will make them free."

"Free! His spirit will set him free so he can fully enjoy his money out of love."

"Can Justice exist in a world plagued with poverty?"

"Poverty is a lack of consciousness in man and the absence of knowledge of your inner self. It is to deny oneself to understand that only human beings conscious of their own worth can be free of this prejudice. Poverty is a prejudice implanted in the subconscious of the poor man who stands aside, keeping himself isolated. How could anyone without his hands eat unless someone helps him? How does anybody get ahead if he doesn't know his own worth?"

"I know my former words to be strong ones but it is time for people to understand that out of this conception and world economic-structure, there is an entire universe conspiring against its own prosperity and its own progressive and self-supportive development, not taking into account that the only thing to do is to know oneself and to make the invaluable and worthwhile things come out."

"What is the difference between a beggar and the president of a corporation?"

"None, from the physical standpoint; they both are human beings with their own mental capacities. They both have feelings, emotions, intelligence, and a definite potential to love and be loved. The fundamental difference lies in that, the president of a corporation truly knows from within that he can achieve anything he is determined to achieve with God's help. It only takes to be aware of that in order to succeed. The rest falls into place by itself and can be learned and used as tools for the achievement of any of man's endeavors. History is filled up with infinite examples like Thomas A. Edison and Jesus, the son of a famous carpenter."

"Then, ethics is to live in society?"

"Let's say that ethics is a living personal experience. Once upon a time, there was a hermit living in a shack somewhere in the woods. He thought he could make it alone on his own. He always said: 'Better alone than with the wrong company.' To such a degree was his solitude; even birds wouldn't come close to him. One day, this hermit got so ill he couldn't move out of bed; all four of his extremities were limp. Right at that moment, he remembered he had a brother somewhere, but in his condition, how could he let anyone know what was going on, if not even birds would fly by near him? Then he remembered there was a God who sees all and started asking him to put him out of his misery so that he would suffer no more. Three days went by and to his surprise, instead of sending death, God sent a boy scout to his aid and the boy scout sent for his owl. Without asking for anything in return, he was carried away to a nearby place for proper health care. In that moment, the hermit realized what had happened, he looked at himself in the mirror and saw the errors and the prejudices that had incurred from his past. Suddenly, he then realized that life is a gift and a responsibility the creator gives us. That the right thing is always in front of our eyes. We only have to open them to see, smell, feel, and live the greatness of the creator within us and everything surrounding us."

"So, what you mean is that a hermit could be anyone who lives in the poverty of the mind, of consciousness, who lives with lack of love and affection. It is not about material wealth, but about knowing that what is right is in the pure heart of human beings."

"You have understood me quite well. You can be wealthy being poor, and can be poor being wealthy, for wealth and poverty are an illusion created by man's lack of consciousness in the principles and potentialities that rule over him. A fair man is wealthy and prosperous; abundance runs like blood trough his veins. An unfair man, on the contrary, will be man's living sadness, a man who never knew where his fundamental wealth truly was."

Thick dark clouds were showing up in the sky as if threatening to rain heavily on us. The proximity of the downpour announced new awakenings. A strange inner-force emerged from Jazmin's innermost place.

"The adventure is just starting," commented Max, Urano, and Dominique. They integrated all the powers of the Universe and swore to stand by Jazmin no matter what. They were committed to travel to The City of Pyramids to face king Cicero, who personified error itself, and his wife, Queen Rebeca, who embodied faith and tenderness and unconditional love, which the king came to learn all about. They begot two daughters and one son, heir to the kingdom... Lucia was more like her father: egotistical and prone to make mistakes. Esperanza was more like her Queen mother. She was Love, faith and hope. Arthur the Future king represented virtue, integrity, union, and rectitude. Arthur the fair was how he was remembered.

Jazmin was about to journey through all her life until the future; she was living every one of those emotions, every one of those times, and she recognized herself and learned to liberate herself of every discordant energy filed away in those memories. She felt much lighter, rid of unwanted luggage and freed from her past. At that moment, she was transported and elevated through an ascended-spiral-energy and her body became transparent and bright. Max, Crosstemps, and Dominique rejoiced, for they knew what was happening to Jazmin. Luminescent crystal-spheres showed up like visions before her and she could see herself as a child. She started linking up to feelings locked away since her childhood and realized her connection to the sphere meant a link to three energies in one: her mind, body, and soul. A very subtle and deep voice seemed to speak out of her heart:

"We shall reveal the truth to you. Everything is a composed of three different energies, which some day will integrate into one. When that occurs, The Man Who Changes The World is born. You are now in the fifth vibrational level. Do not try to imagine its shape; someday you will see it; you are on the way. Soon you, along with humanity, will know God's Divine Plan. Life is but a trip to space through the tunnel of light that goes across all astral planes. The Man Who Changes The World is a sublime energy that reaches the hearts of every living being. You are only a marvelous instrument of God's Plan, remembering the right path. God has spoken to you today. Don't ever doubt it. Your wealth and prosperity are guaranteed, and your family is your great support and stronghold."

Sighing deeply in ecstasy and feeling the warmth of the sun upon her young face, Jazmin finished this marvelous encounter with The Tree of Justice. Very closely, near her, Crosstemps, Max, and Dominique were sleeping like rocks, while Mr. Way opening his arms, was very grateful for the sun of a new day.

THE TREE OF TRUTHFULNESS

"You are here to find out your mission, right?", Mr. Way inquired.

"Of course, indeed. What I wish the most right now is to know the way that will take me to my grandfather, to meet the man that changes the world, and to find the password to access The City of Pyramids. Every time I remember grandpa's stories, I ask myself, how was it possible that men regretted breathing?"

"I wish it had never happened," Mr. Way said. "But you can remedy it."

"I am afraid I am not wise enough," she said with an expression of respect on her face.

"Why not?", he inquired. "With enough faith, you can remedy it."

"Yes", Jazmin answered. "But faith is a consequence of knowing the right way of things. Wise men have got that level of knowledge and I would like to reach that kind of knowledge now."

"Very well. Close your eyes. Breathe slowly and gently nine times. Inhale and pay attention to the sound of nature. Exhale and fill the woods with your breath. Let yourself expand your presence and vitality. Dance with the breeze and feel the earth pulsating under your feet. Allow your heart to discover The Tree of truthfulness and embrace yourself to him to receive his energy and the wisdom you want."

Jazmin was familiar with all these stories because her grandpa Ezequiel would tell them at sunset just before he would watch the sacred energy. Now she was able to confirm that beauty and happiness do expand before all of us and only those who seek the Creator in their hearts have the privilege to interview a sage. She hugged the giant tree who seemed generous and kind. His huge branches extended, as if reaching out to embrace the wind in an endless, inexhaustible love that had maintained happiness in spite of men having forgotten how to love and share.

"I greet the truth in you with unconditional love from the memory of everything and everyone."

"Hello," Jazmin greeted happily.

"I am going to share an enjoyable story with you. It is the story of a planet that turned around in circles without stopping. Everything in it happened in tune with people's lives, and with plants, animals, and everything that could breathe. It was simple: to inhale and accept what the heart says; to exhale and multiply all we are; an easy task occurring twenty-four hours a day each day, from Sunday to Sunday."

"Ah, I know what you mean." Jazmin said.

"One day," the Tree of Truthfulness continued, "some men who did not believe that things were easy and fun to do decided to sow the seeds of doubt, and these started to grow and expand in a menacing way. They seized all those beings who had left happiness and had stopped believing, from listening to too many of people's stories to pretending to agree with incredulous people. This changed the planet's rhythm, and everything was turning sad because everyone started to be fearsome and began to breath differently. These people thought and came to believe that laughter was a lack of seriousness. If anyone were to be talking and having a good laugh, they would ask him: really? Or is that true? Time had changed everything. Men stopped appreciating beauty, because they converted to pessimism, worshiping it on a daily basis. No longer could they listen to the melodies of nature, nor sense the fresh smell of the woods, which at times, carried the words old sages gave as gifts, though the wind. Then, trees started dreaming."

"Can trees dream?", Jazmin questioned.

"You still doubt it," the Tree of Truthfulness stated in grief.

"I dream of the Grand Day that men once again recognize their truth, for love and truthfulness are the same thing. Truth and love never lie because they hold within them the integrity of forgiveness. Truth and love come to be through happiness."

"Some things are hard to forgive. What about unfair deaths, dire poverty, or war?"

"That occurs because you are looking at these events through the lens of fear. True forgiveness is to never have to forgive because truthfulness is recognized in the inexhaustible and the eternal. It is like breathing freely at dawn on a green field. I came to the world; one day, the creator brought out from the midst of his loving heart, live seeds. He scattered them throughout the world by blowing them off with his breath. We were about one hundred and forty-four thousand in number and started to grow in the woods, knowing that one day, the soul of an innocent girl would embrace us to listen to our blessings and receive the light to accomplish her sacred mission."

A cascade of light that flowed from the heart of The Tree of Truthfulness bathed Jazmin. She received the truthfulness baptism in the woods of Little San Juan. Since then, her old view of the world went away to never return again.

She was ready to rediscover with happiness her natural gifts within The Trees of Wisdom.

THE TREE OF COMMON GOOD

An enormously giant being communicated with Jazmin every time she'd hug one of the trees. What she perceived was to feel from planet earth, its love, and understanding. Once again, the awareness of life, feelings, and how goodness made itself present the more her consciousness penetrated a different realm, and she thought to herself:

"Men will only be able to love; the moment they understand the real magnitude of this story and like me, they come into the light." She heard a whispering voice say:

"I am the Tree of Common Good. One day, I separated from my father, The Tree of Good, in the form of a seed," The Tree of Common Good said. "My father, the great sage, had a mastery in the knowledge of the profound and sincere wishes of human beings on the things they consider valuable, useful, and important. These things are part of his nature and that's the reason for men wishing them so much. I learned everything I know from my father and chose to be a master of **Common Good** to know the necessary conditions to develop man's life and fate in society."

"So, you didn't come from the heart of God?", Jazmin said in amazement.

"Yes; but God's paths are infinite, and out of his unlimited kindness, he let me choose my father as a vehicle. I am sure the same thing happened to you and whenever you wish, you'll delve into your heart to retrieve that particular memory."

"I love that you are here with me, because I love teaching everything I've learned, and I deeply appreciate you being the one to let me know the reason for my existence," Jazmin said.

41

"I am happy too; you seem to be funny and your presence inspires happiness in me."

"It is marvelous to be before a giant dreamer who fills my spirit of self-esteem. I want to know all the conditions for a human being to develop his destiny in society," Jazmin said right away.

"There are nine principles. Freedom of thought and action is the first condition. That means honoring free will. Leading to an end through definite rules for the development of the individual and the collective mass of society members. It is like a roadmap that everyone can understand to follow a route leading to a common destination. A guarantee of security, peace, tranquility, and political stability. This is the way to love your neighbor. Guaranteeing equal and fair access to all individuals in the development of their own personality in society as a consequence of exercising respect for the universality of perceptions expressed by the individual. Guide and facilitate the organization of the communities in order to develop and solve specific problems in the community. This means that everyone assumes their mission with love. Clearly establish channels of communication in the inter-subjective relationships between the citizens themselves and the state. This means opening the channels for a real communion between all members in the project and achieving compromise from the members of the society involved in the regional and national projects. This requires full knowledge of their abilities and virtues. Establish the framework of individual and collective certainty in regard to micro and macro guidelines in society. It is the integrity applied to the realization of a common project and it has to do with the intentions of the heart. To achieve a sense of belonging in the society members necessary for individual and collective development. It is the recognition of self as an integral part of the one and all."

"That sounds interesting, but do I have to go through all that to find the man that changes the world? Is the password the key to reach it? When will I finally get to find my grandfather?", Jazmin interrogated.

Once again, uncertainty made her breathing pattern change. She could no longer be able to listen to the wise words of the woods. That feeling brought the magical experience to an abrupt end. Next thing, it became dark, and the sadness returned in Jazmin.

On the morning of San Juan's day, Jazmin woke up at the same time as the others and started having breakfast trying to disguise her sadness and hide it from her friends.

"We brought you a ton of fresh fruits," Max told her.

"Yeah, that's good," Jazmin said sadly.

"Sit down," Mr. Way said while observing the scene. Jazmin turned to look at him and his eyes were sparkling.

"You think you cannot face the obstacles," The Lord of The Woods started saying.

"Yes, I think that it was easier for me to accept the fact that I will never see my grandparents again. The police were right! All this is no more than a fantasy. Perhaps what is required is a Forestry Service to control all the walkers that come to the forest and that's it! You do not exist, neither does this forest, nor Max. Dominique neither lives nor flies and Crosstemps is a fallacy," she said, tearful, desperate, and running out into the woods. She ran until she was exhausted and tripped over something that made her fall on her face. There, she was crying for a while, liberating, flowing with her once repressed feelings. All of a sudden, she sat up, seeing everything with an unusually sharp clarity; all the colors were more brilliant and luminescent. The magnificent view filled her with courage, and she said, "I can't stay here any longer, I've got to get back," and shutting her eyes, she breathed nine times and felt how little by little, her own energy was raising to another level. This time, it had been a lot easier, and her friends reappeared before her.

"Mr. Way, I'm really embarrassed," she said trembling.

"It is good to express ourselves," Mr. Way replied to her remark. "Emotions are sacred valves through which God manifests in each one of us. When we hold back on our feelings, they get transformed into all kinds of tangible obstacles; our breathing changes and we start to see everything through fear." He then asked her: "What is it you wish to do now?"

"Continue with my mission; but tell me, how is it that this time it was so much easier to get back to you?"

"Well, there are many special places within these woods, which help make your wishes come true. They are dimensional portals aligned to the wisdom of your heart and the images of your thoughts."

"But, how will I know if I am in a special place?"

"Do you remember why we are all here together in the first place? Allow your heart to provide you with the answer while you breathe. You'll be able to understand it along the way."

THE TREE OF UNCONDITIONAL LOVE

This time, Jazmin had banished all her fears away. She knew she had to go on and went still deeper into the forest about 1900 feet. Now freed from her visceral feelings, she was ready to listen to the voice of the wind, which would indicate where to go, and where she was to find The Tree of Unconditional Love. This Tree would obviously reveal to her the reason for finding this dimensional portal, giving her new significant information to continue with the adventure. An intense sensation of having been in that very spot of the forest arose in her mind. She remembered a crystal-clear lagoon and noticed the sound of a waterfall in the background. Once again, she experienced anxiety. Suddenly, she was startled by an animal that took off running. It turned out to be a large, white rabbit.

She tried to glimpse in between the trees. One tree caught her attention; it was a leafless tree, where crows were nestling. There were lots of willow trees and a number of large palm trees. About some sixty feet away, to her right, she could see a smooth hill. At the top of this hill, three wonderful trees were standing. This seemed like the perfect place for her to reflect for a while. She walked over and settled in right between them, sitting with her back leaning against the trunk of one of the trees. She could spend many days in there. *What sense did the image of the tree and the crows have?* Jazmin thought to herself and closed her eyes. She breathed deeply once again and looked at the magnificence of the forest and the flowers, sensing the water flowing from the waterfall all the way into the lake. Whispering voices were heard like background music flowing to the rhythm of the water. Then she heard a voice clearly state:

"I am the essence of the living God, now and ever," interrupted the Tree she was leaning up against. She kept on saying, "I greet within you all those human beings who are eternal light recognized through all time. I am the very essence of omnipresent love within all things."

"Hello!", said a somewhat afraid Jazmin. "I'm searching for the password to go to The City of Pyramids. I want to meet The Man Who Changes The World and find my Grandpa. Can you help me?"

"I like knowing that the day is coming in which men will walk as a group towards the same dawn without any fears. That they are open now to verify the truth of their hearts."

"How do you achieve Unconditional Love?", Jazmin questioned.

"Simplicity and Humbleness are the ways to attain it. It is simple: to love by loving; to feel by feeling; to live by living; to smile by smiling; to be yourself by being; to share by sharing. It is to be and be happy."

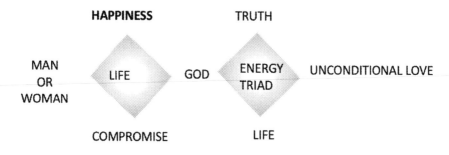

"What does it mean to love unconditionally?"

"To love is to live life intensely. To love is to feel that all or nothing matters. It is to think that good is within another human being. It is to melt into the smile of a child or into a mother's caress. It is to know that hate does not exist, since it is just an illusion of those who have not learned to love. It is to understand that the goal, meaning, and purpose of everything is that The Light of God be with you.

Only with love in the heart can poetry, beauty, and the melody of the universe emerge. Only with love in the heart do we successfully get out of combat. Blessed are you, for your mission is to be both the loving and the beloved. Soon the sun will rise again, and the brilliant sun of love will celebrate that once again it has overcome the boundaries of darkness. Only through unconditional love can you listen to the musicality of the universe."

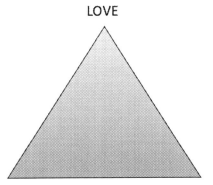

THE TREE OF INTEGRITY

For a moment, everything seemed to be gray and lugubrious. The birds would not sing and the usual joy present at dawn was missing. Today is a day just as the one in which God started to check his heart and armed himself with all kinds of colors, birds, flowers, precious stones, lakes, and waterfalls. He opened up a small place within his heart to make sure that while it beat, everything would be watered with love, sweetness, and wisdom. He knew exactly what he wanted to do. Just like love, he wanted to expand himself to the rhythm of the universal vibration, bringing nature into existence. She is the mother of a giant who would sometimes seem to be asleep and forgotten for thousands of years. This is The Tree of Integrity.

"That's how Grandpa would tell the story of The Tree of Integrity," Jazmin said.

"Then you grew up and thought that they were 'just stories that grandpa was telling you.' And as you can see," said Mr. Way, "You are about to listen to the message this giant of The Cosmos, The Tree of Integrity, is going to share with you."

The light breeze suddenly accelerated its own rhythm, transforming itself into a strong wind announcing rain or something transcendental. Right before Jazmin's eyes, thousands and thousands of light sparks, tiny, small, big…huge, were floating in the atmosphere and formed some kind of door. Jazmin closed her eyes and went confidently towards that door. A tunnel of light filled with stars that resembled little girls on their school break, playing hide-and-seek throughout the universe and hiding behind the planets. She could breathe peace, equilibrium, and perfection. She was in a different kind of universe or perhaps in an earlier stage of the one she knew well. All days and nights were still within God's heart, since the sun was still a project to be completed. Yet, Joy was still needed for the sun to be born. It was still in the long dream of gestation. Integrity is light; it is clarity.

"Soon the light will be born." A voice was heard from the end of the tunnel. Jazmin opened her eyes; she was astonished. She remembered the creation of The Sun and saw The Tree of Integrity right in front of her. It emerged, showing its branches full of tiny leaves and yellow flowers, the likes of which no one had ever seen. It was growing and growing filling the planets up with light, overshadowing, even if for the span of a second, the brightest of stars.

She felt her heart beating as her body was impregnated with that powerful, vital energy, overflowing with enormous light-waves. That light was well kept within her and its reappearance was not a coincidence, since in order to be able to find Ezequiel, she would have to clearly see the path and create, from light, unconditional love. A thunderous lightning-like voice emerged out of the heart of the woods.

"I greet the truth living within you and bless your capacity to create all the beautiful things that dwell within you," said the magnificent Tree of Integrity, giving some of his own flowers to Jazmin. She just stared with great love and with the certainty of having been fully identified with that infinite totality, which she was just beginning to understand.

Nevertheless, the way of the road was not completely clear, Jazmin was making her descent towards a beautiful place, through a spiral-like path made out of stardust coming abundantly out of the heart of The Creator. The more flowers that would fall out of The Tree of Integrity on the path, the wider the path would get; so much so, that even stars, planets, and love itself would be able to go down through it. All the animals of the forest, the flowers, and the trees now knew the magic of Integrity, which lets you appreciate the truth of things.

Everything exists thanks to The Light. Lacking is a product of darkness and a projection out of fear. Plants are green thanks to the sun and the light; because of them, fruits and flowers are produced. They are the cause of all life and without that light, life perishes. Businesses perish when they move away from the light and when they project their lives through fear and darkness. When humanity recognizes and accepts the light and the truth about things, all will be transformed into prosperity. Now you have learned an old lesson. Follow the wish of your heart and you'll be able to meet The Tree of Intuition so that you may vibrate forever within the high frequency of love and integrity.

THE TREE OF INTUITION

A new mystery was in front of Jazmin. She had to find The Tree of Intuition in the forest within the forest. Grandpa Ezequiel had always said that anyone who eats the fruit of this Tree becomes wise. I was convinced that these fruits had to be delicious, like the pies that Grandma Rosa would bake every afternoon. She walked aimlessly, following the yellow flowers, and finally came to a leafy tree and hugged it tight.

"Are you The Tree of Intuition?", Jazmin asked. "Why do you ask if you already know it?", The Tree grumbled. "I am sorry; I didn't mean to bother you. It is just that I am looking for my grandpa and have to go through all the nine Trees before I can defeat Midas and enter The City of Pyramids, where my grandpa is, and where I will find and rescue The Sacred Password."

"Bah! That is an adventure for brave people only! Not for foolish little girls like you," The Tree said. For a moment, I doubted. The Huge Tree had some nice-looking fruits, but his gestures were so hateful that he could not be The Tree of Intuition. After all, a sage couldn't be all that unfriendly, so I started to walk away from the giant. "Wait up, you foolish little one! I believe you have forgotten to ask your heart; do you think you will always have someone whispering all the answers in your ears?", replied The Tree. "Fine; what makes you think that I have to put up with the irrelevant remarks of a wrinkled old tree?"

"Me, old and wrinkled?" He immediately bent down his long branches to see his own reflection into the lake, and tears sprang out of his trunk, so many of them, that it seemed like a winter rain. Jazmin felt embarrassed and tried to apologize.

"Well, I didn't mean it . . . it's fine, you are tall and beautiful I must admit; I just wanted to teach you a lesson."

53

"Seriously? Do you really think that I am beautiful?" The Tree asked.

"Of course, I think you are beautiful; now, tell me, do you know where I could find The Tree of Intuition?"

"I am he; it is just that people no longer call upon me, and I've almost forgotten what my job is about."

"Then, I gather intuition could be capricious and whining."

"Indeed, we are beings just like you; we have feelings and we like compliments. I am intuition, the fountain of wisdom of all time. Each one of my folds can tell ancient-thousand-year-old-stories, ever since the sun came into existence for the first time."

"Is it true that he who eats of your fruit?"

"Oh yes! And I must warn you that once you eat of this fruit, you will have, just as me, all the knowledge there is, and unless you so choose, it is impossible for you to err on your choices and paths; in view of the fact that even in choosing by mistake, you will always be right, since in the end, you will eventually learn some lesson of it."

"I'd like to have some; are they sweet?"

"They have all the flavors as all lessons in life. Sometimes they are sweet; other times they are bitter; some are sour, and others are bland. It is a matter of perception; what is tasty for you may not taste so good for someone else."

Immediately, a shower of fruits fell on Jazmin and her friends because The Tree of Intuition is also mischievous. She picked up some and tasted them. They did have different flavors. Every time she tasted one of them, a dormant memory would wake up from the past. It was just all those pending matters she had to work out with her loved ones, her city, her friends, and the world she had chosen to grow in. She accepted that ego is an integral part of wisdom and that the illusion of separation is one of the paths towards unity. She then understood that her encounter with The Trees of Forgiveness, Compassion, and Gratitude was imminent.

THE TREE OF FORGIVENESS

This time, in the woods of Little San Juan, The Master Trees were greeting Jazmin in the distance, showing themselves very easily before her.

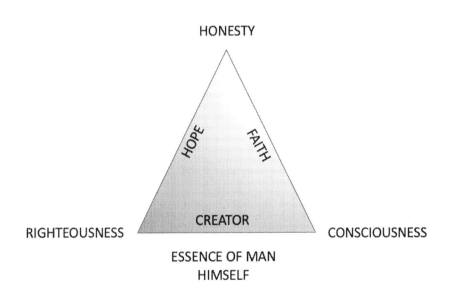

She was surprised when she realized that she no longer had to make any efforts to find and contact them. They looked at her from afar and greeted her. That is exactly the way it happened with The Tree of Forgiveness. "Hey, here I am!", a voice in the middle of a group of trees shouted. "Over here to your right. It is I, the one with the blue jay nest and the violet flowers. Ah, at last you can see me! How would you like to try my fruits?", spoke the leafy Tree of forgiveness.

"Well, maybe," said Jazmin. "Are they sweet?"

"Always the same; people want for the fruits of forgiveness to be sweet," he said in a boring tone of voice. "But all they have in their saliva to combine is bitter. So, how do they expect to taste the sweetness in anything? For more than five thousand years, I've offered people my fruits without expecting anything in return other that they benefit from them, because they are the secret of health, beauty, and a plentiful life. But everyone continues to look for sweetness through bitterness." The millenary Tree expressed all of this in obvious discontent. "Sorry, I mean, forgive me, I didn't mean to turn down your offer," Jazmin said blushing.

"Forgiveness and love are subtle essences that can do everything," said The Tree of Forgiveness, who then sighed. Dominique, Max, and Crosstemps were happy to see him again. They always said that their dreams had come true after having eaten from The Tree of Forgiveness, even though it was difficult to digest its fruits, but it was truly miraculous.

"Forgiveness is an act of tenderness; it is a feeling of kind love and sensitivity. Life is love, and forgiveness is a sublime, purifying, intense, deeply harmonious love, with the power to change anything and everything," said the thick-leafy Tree of Forgiveness with its purple flowers.

"Love is the fundamental basis of human beings and is represented by a blue ray. Forgiveness is represented by a violet ray. The essence of love is the center of The Universe and the essence of the Universe is God, who is love and creative energy.

"Forgiveness is a gift of the creative energy that is God. It is your Alpha and your Omega, past and future. It is the difference between life and death. God is living, feeling, and sharing. God is loving the good, the simple, the easy, and the humble. God is you yourself in your own divine essence, and within your divine essence is forgiveness.

"I am going to tell you a story: One day, Jesus was on the road and someone asked him: 'Who is the wisest man on this world?' Since he was wise, he took a few seconds to respond and then said

'He, who in his own humbleness, knows that God knows everything and sees everything.' Wisdom comes from God; therefore, God is the wisest on heaven and earth. Simply, man is an instrument of his intelligence and wisdom. An old master used to say: 'A man who recognizes his own limitations is a wise being, because he knows that from that point, he can reach the unlimited in God.' Love is the deep-solid rock on which this world was erected."

"Then, what is forgiveness?"

"It is love as an unlimited action of the creator. It is a sublime, broad, dynamic, and intelligent energy movement, which can change and transform anything and everything. It is the odyssey between good and evil and the magic of a bipolar world that gives us the possibility to grow and be better. Love is the reason and foundation of everything. It is the essence of life and dwells within each and every one of us. You and I are a part of it now and always. Life is light and love. That is the reason the soul exists; and he who hates dies in life. Forgiving is the greatest gift of love and to love means to forgive. Now you are now ready to meet compassion."

THE TREE OF COMPASSION

While admiring the beautiful view, the unusually rare sensation was growing. All the sounds, the colors, the grass, everything was becoming increasingly familiar to Jazmin. She had been in this place before; she was remembering it, but when was this? She was feeling tender warmth she had not experienced in years. It was an almost-forgotten emotion that she was now recognizing perfectly. She opened her eyes and turned around halfway, certain that she was going to find someone. Right then, she started to see some images, some of which were from other times. She was able to observe a great battle where she was victorious, and she hugged her Grandpa after releasing him from captivity.

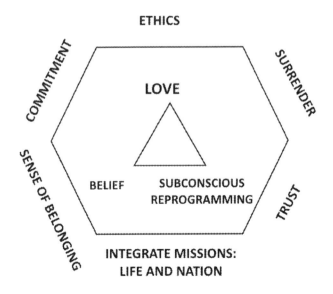

Jazmin was picking up images of things yet to come. Crosstemps, who knew very well every inch, every detail, and every corner within the line of time, told her: "Had you let those images fade away, I would have certainly thought that your faith would have been out of tune and eventually lost. But I see that you have taken the revelation very seriously and made it stronger in your thought."

"Why did I see all those images from other times, some of them from the past?"

"In other dimensions, you live anther life. When you are afraid you back away from that vibrational frequency. When you enjoy and love beauty, you raise your vibrational frequency and experience an incredible world where you can move anywhere in the universe simply by imagining the places."

"What happens when my mind imagines a huge bright-white screen?"

"You go into the dimension of pure ideas and innocence, where you may create everything you want to create, and accomplish big negotiations with important people."

"Could it be boring to create the world just as you want it? What would happen to surprises?"

"You may feel satisfaction, but not total inner plenitude, since you would be too controlling and lose your path by losing your evolving emotion and experiencing harmony with other human beings in nature."

"What is the password?"

"Look inside yourself the door of entry to a higher dimension that leads directly to The Divine Father and The Divine Mother in the way you already know. It is like floating upwards, ascending until you reach the vibration of other souls and groups of souls in order to grasp their thoughts and wisdom. They will show you the true sense of Compassion."

"Wait a minute now. The souls from that dimension will be the ones taking me to The Tree of Compassion?"

"Yes, because they will show you the process of being born as well as the process of dying; where we come from and how to accomplish your mission by letting you see God's Divine Plan, which we are a part of. This is because man's evolution occurs out of compassion, which is a point of view of other dimensions, and it is the cause that some eternal beings make both dimensions merge. Man's common mission is to help integrate the two dimensions. You will get to know The Tree of Compassion once you are ready for a new spiritual consciousness."

Crosstemps came to an abrupt stop; he looked around in expectation and said, "Did you hear that?"

I tried, but I could only hear the crickets. "I have heard that sound before; what is it?"

"I don't know, but it sounds like that in the higher planes as well," said Crosstemps with a spaced out look on his face. He turned and contemplated the marvelous scenery while we talked and said, "If we both concentrate very intently on The Tree of Compassion, we could bring him down to our dimension; let's breathe." We started breathing deeply and little by little. Crosstemps' figure was somewhat out of focus, and while facing each other, we exchanged energies through our respective solar plexuses. The intensity of the strange sound was increasing like thunder and the ground was quaking as the humongous tree was emerging out of the center of the earth. The immense crack revealed that the center of the earth is made of quartz and light.

It was then that Jazmin understood that compassion has no words to describe it, since it is such a high message that it can only be transmitted from heart to heart. It is an energy born out of intention and identified through peace and intuition, persuading us into recognizing the power within others to create through faith. We may love and create at the same time. We can all do it when we are harmonized and when we see true intent within the heart. An array of multicolored rainbow-like energies launched Jazmin and her friends through a kind of a bright tunnel at breathtaking speed all the way through the woods. She asked herself: *why didn't she feel fear?* On the contrary, there was only peace and happiness in all her sensations and when they came to a stop, they were surrounded by a pure, brilliant, warm light. She descended on the branches of an enormous tree with wonderful fruits and flowers sprouting all around it. A voice was heard; "I am The Tree of Gratitude," he introduced himself.

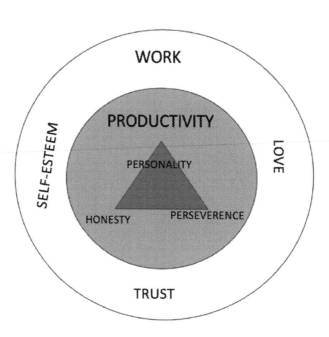

THE TREE OF GRATITUDE

"How can you make so many fruits and flowers so quickly?", Jazmin interrogated.

"Every time a human being is thankful about something, my fruits multiply to fill the earth with everything humanity could possibly wish for."

The Tree of Gratitude seemed to smile, and I saw the light shining from within the tree. I was touching his branches as I was sliding down towards the prairie and I noticed how my body was just as bright as the tree's. Then I came to understand that I was a part of that energy being able to even go inside him since we are not really separated.

"This is the highest vibration," I pointed out to Mr. way. "Where are we? How come there is no horizon?"

"How would you know that the vibration is low?", asked The Tree of Gratitude.

"Because then, there would be an above and a below, and below, I would be devoid of energy and light. Perhaps this incredible experience wouldn't even be happening now."

"Exactly, very good," said The Tree of Gratitude. "Things occur the same way above and below. Whenever people stop being grateful, the vital energy in me is reduced, and along with that, so is The Divine Providence that I Am. The more gratitude that comes out of the heart, and even more if it is expressed through unconditional love, the larger my blessings will be." Now Jazmin came to understand why suddenly, one day, men had lost the ability to perform miracles. She assumed the gift of command, true leadership, and by loving the entire universe, she started to love and forgive and spread wisdom.

More than two thousand years had passed by before Jazmin once again would start to verify all the truths in her heart. Such truths have been with her since the beginning of time within the ever-present infinity. Then she realized that very soon, she would be able to create her own truths, her own emotions, and the marvelous surroundings she deserved to live in. She could do these and even more by just tuning in with the musicality of the universe and the beauty within her own self.

Once again, it was almost dawn, and Jazmin had all the tools she needed to meet and defeat Midas, enter The City of Pyramids, find her Grandpa' Ezequiel, and discover The Sacred Password to meet The Man that Changes The World.

PART FIVE

INTERNAL CHAOS

GENERAL MIDAS

All colors seemed to be more intense, turning iridescent as Jazmin and her friends went deeper into that scenery full of wild flowers and branchy trees with rough barks, some of them exposing their cortexes sprinkled with amber and multiple hues. The more she breathed, the higher she tuned in with nature. Jazmin kneeled behind some bushes and through the foliage; she could distinguish a lone figure that was observing all around.

She thought to herself, *who are these people?* Her first impulse was to run away, but her heart just knew that there were no alternatives. She shut her eyes and once again remembered Mr. Way's advice and tried to keep a fixed image of a bright light in her mind. Out of nowhere, the loud shriek of a bird was heard; it was a large eagle flying through the air towards the north. The sudden appearance sharpened Jazmin's intuition, and somehow, it increased her level of energy.

Then quickly, her mind went to another time and place into a scene happening within a parallel existence. She saw lit torches and preliminary plans for a full-scale military attack. Disagreement prevailed on the atmosphere and the hope for peace was totally lost. War was about to break loose. Jazmin felt all her energies depleting from the anguish she felt while trying to keep her thoughts centered in beauty and love. Very close by, Mr. Way, Urano, Crosstemps, Dominique, and Max observed silently, for they knew that in order for Jazmin to find The Sacred Password, it was necessary for her to face and confront power.

They had gone into Midas' tenebrous territory. He was the guardian of the boundary towards The City of Pyramids. This boundary between the real and the unreal was the place where everything was prone to change through manipulation and control to favor the obscure interests of those who made possible and caused poverty, insecurity; and where those most needy were in no way, allowed to decide for themselves.

That was the terrifying picture Jazmin and her friends encountered and had to overcome; since there, fantasy and reality were easily confused, and their lives could be at risk. Jazmin knew that war pleased those who were in control. She also knew that it was there where important changes in regard to their viewpoint could be made. Was she starting to understand that her mission was that of convincing the great chiefs of the world to get together with the purpose of getting into an agreement of sharing and reconciliation?

Jazmin could visualize the great battle's scenario. Heavy cavalry appeared on top of the hill and a group of soldiers posted behind the rocks, were thinking about defending themselves from enemies they once called brothers.

Something inside their hearts desperately cried out because they were convinced that somehow, they didn't have to live through any war, since there is always a way to be integrated to evolve.

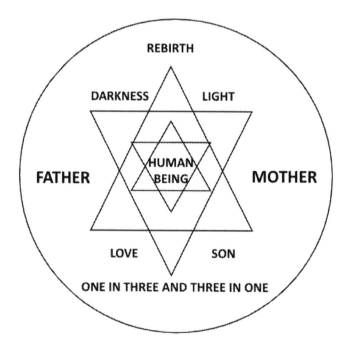

Jazmin had already made up her mind about not giving up, at least until she could put an end to violence. So, she kept repeating without stopping: "It can be settled! It can be settled!"

The horror of hate and bloodshed was starting to break out again, and Jazmin knew that the fact of not having stopped all this on time was the basis for conflict. But just as before, she wasn't awake, and she had to do her best to help dissipate fear. Now she could understand how fear was the hidden enemy and the cause that men were only aware of and living within just one plane of existence. This gave those who controlled the main roll time, which legitimately belonged to love. Jazmin trembled out of anxiety when she came to realize the importance of her mission and how urgent it was to gather up her groups to combine wills and efforts in order to re-conquer those spaces still in the hands of fear.

"What's wrong?", Dominique asked.

"I experienced a vision of the future. Do you know what it is about?"

"Yes, of course!", Dominique replied. "It is the broadened consciousness during this trip that has put in front of you the great shock that fear generates in men. This knowledge compromises us, since we would never want to go through the suffering and pain of looking back some day and realize that we did wrong; that we didn't make the right decision, nor did we act in accordance with our mission."

Unexpectedly, Dominique stopped talking and raised his head. At that instant, he felt once again the pressure in the middle of the stomach while hearing that weird sound. The sky turned dark gray. What was happening was directly affecting the dimension they were in now. A thundering sound burst into Jazmin's body and knocked her down to the ground. She tried to keep a firm grip on the branches, but her strength failed her, and she fell through a tunnel amid a landscape of different hues of gray.

While rolling down to the bottom in a seemingly endless route, she remembered Mr. Way's favorite words: "Breathe slowly and rhythmically; it is perfectly safe to breathe." She did just that, and little by little, she rid herself of the vertigo and found herself faced with the beautiful landscape of the woods, and her bag was right where she had left it. She looked around. It had been a nightmare, but it was different from the others in that it happened while she was wide awake.

What had happened? Where had her faithful friends gone to? How much time had passed by since they had entered that dimension? She was exhausted and picked her back up while still feeling a knot of fear inside her throat and her stomach tight. She started walking downhill when she saw a man of about fifty years of age, wearing a cloak that reminded her of medieval times. The man saw Jazmin before she could hide, and he started to walk towards her. Her intuition told her that she was at the exact time and place to gain a great knowledge that would determine the course of this adventure.

The strange person seemed very sure of himself and approached her with firm steps, observing every detail.

"You wouldn't be intending to get to The City of Pyramids, would you?", he questioned her, trying to disguise the rage evidenced on his face since the beginning of time.

"Perhaps, and why not?", Jazmin replied in between fear and apprehension.

"What are you are you doing wandering around this place?" His tone indicated that he was used to addressing people in a direct way.

"It occurs to me that I want to do some tourism; that's it! Forest tourism!", she said, trying to be as nice as she could possibly be.

"Oh, really? And, what is it you expect to find?"

"I'll walk until I find a mystical place."

"Oh, I see… searching for utopias!"

She understood that he was fishing around to see if she would fall for it. "I take it you don't believe in utopias, unicorns, and other dimensions, right?"

"No, of course not; it is ridiculous to think about things like that. That is what I call naïve, Neanderthal thinking. No marvel awaits us. Everything just happens; it is all going bad and it is getting worse. As time goes by, there is less and less money and people just want to explode," said the man.

"Why do you say that, Mr.…? Excuse me, … you didn't tell me your name, did you?"

"General Midas; King Cicero's Special Commissioner to the Forestry Guard of these woods. I am responsible for everything within this universe to be reasonably kept within the framework of logic and its laws. Those who have must be kept apart from those who don't, period! Those who invest, we keep them close by; and those who do all the dirty work… over there."

"It sounds really awful that you would want to keep things that way, separated and divided," Jazmin pointed out.

"That is realistic. Separation is the truth of the majority. Those who want to survive have to make an effort until they burst. Don't you ever read those surveys on stress? Crime rate increases. Law, order and human rights are disappearing. Envy and revenge have changed people and have made the world a better place for me. How about that, huh?"

Jazmin caught her breath back and looked at him. She'd realized that she let herself be dragged down by the gray atmosphere and that perverse discourse had already started to sound familiar. One question kept echoing inside her head: *what is the purpose of me running into this man?* The answer didn't wait to hit her. She was faced with the vision of fear Mr. Way had mentioned when they started the journey. Having realized this, she started trembling, since this was really supposed to happen because she knew that if she were to overcome this trial, she would be allowed to enter The City of Pyramids and find her Grandpa.

Jazmin replied, "It seems to me that things are very much different. I will soon be a lawyer and I've known about this kind of attitude in the professional atmosphere; for instance, I know that some lawyers act that way. There used to be a time when we tried our very best to do our job with a certain criterion of ethics and integrity, but not anymore. Nowadays, it all comes down to presupposing guilt, litigation and sensationalism. Sometimes, it would seem as if people no longer look for justice, truth, and common good."

"Well, well… I see you were talking with those fossils about all those summer fantasies."

"Yes, indeed, I have, and I'll tell you right now that for some time, it was significantly good to be a member of The Court, since both parts had respect for truth and justice. Now you see how they use TV shows as a means of showing off and where the protagonists are all celebrities. Many lawyers would do anything to corrupt justice with the purpose of convincing judges to believe in hypotheses lacking real evidence and proof. They know they are lying on purpose in order to let someone free, and their colleagues make comments on the procedures they use as if these were valid ones in a right-hood state, which is very wrong."

"Oh, … The revolutionary girl that changes the world!", said Midas in a mocking tone of voice.

"Maybe, but all I'm saying is that we need a system were every person has the right to a fair trial. Everyone must be responsible for justice to be made and for the correct application of the law, with truth being the main objective, as opposed to asking for higher fees, to set someone who doesn't deserve to be free, or to be famous and simply turn ourselves into opportunists. Many of us care to preserve the spirit of trust within society."

The General was answering all of these questions and was starting to accept all of them, while he was getting smaller and smaller.

"Ah, hah! And do you, foolish little woman, believe that with some kind of spiritual trickery, you could change the state of things?", asked General Midas, in between ironic laughter.

"That is what I hope will happen, and not precisely because of some scheme, as you say, but because of ethics and true justice."

"Enough of that! You, foolish little woman," shouted the General. "You listen to me and listen to me good! For a long time, I believed in that you call spirituality, in the destiny of the universe, and the purpose of humanity. All of that is crazy. The mind of man can imagine all kinds of nonsense; all of it is just fantasy. The truth lies within reason and logic, the demonstrable and the dominion of the strongest, the most skillful, the most astute."

Jazmin just listened and followed her heart, breathing with the trustworthy image of her grandfather alive in her memory. She watched the forest and the bushes all around. She was convinced that something unexpected was about to happen, while General Midas was ranting and raving, criticizing the system of things and slowly getting sad.

Her mood changed and for some strange reason, Jazmin could see how the halo of energy around the man diminished, gaps were opened, and he soon began to look tired, exhausted, and weak. She watched and breathed, focusing on her heart and the memories of peace that inhabited in her mind. Midas was tired, and Jasmin questioned him.

"General, do you believe in God?"

"If it exists, it must be a monstrous guy," Midas replied mournfully, still looking at the ground. "It has to be too cruel. It is too much to see the world full of wars, children dying of hunger, crime, and hunger while a few throw food away and manufacture weapons."

Maybe that's the way it should be. Maybe that is God's plan. Maybe it will happen until men accept their responsibility in it.

"Is it a Divine plan to end humanity?", he grinned maliciously, as he immediately vanished the gesture.

I stopped and looked at him. He had a swaggering and macho attitude that conjugated with false airs of heroism. I just listened to him carefully, because behind all that armor was hidden a being that cried out from his heart the return to his essence, to his true power. I felt compassion while listening to him renege.

"Even the ancient scriptures in their prophecies speak of destruction, giant earthquakes, the collapse of the economies, floods of the seas, and the emergence of a politician who will propose a plan to accommodate everything again from the Supreme Power. That is a spiritual utopia. Only ambition and corruption will take power."

"Is that the reality of the situation you want to live?", questioned Jazmin.

"How would you like things to be? Could it be that you are living insincerely in some aspect of the reality that you live? How much responsibility do you have that the world is like this?"

The General responded to these questions and accepted, while he was growing small. Meanwhile, Midas accepted the situation and chose how he would like things to be. His energy changed, and little by little, he became conscious.

Time passed by, and he was committed to do something that would transform the situation, contributing with himself to make his dreams come true. Tears came out of his eyes, and as I looked deep into his eyes, I could see the innocent heart of a child someday returning back home. Jazmin was listening to the beat of The Earth, looking around the surrounding space and focusing her attention on the light. She just knew that the former General Midas, and all of his discourse, was merely a projection of his fears, and that if she focused on the light, it would increase the level of the vibration. As she breathed, she was going up higher, with her stare fixed on love, while Midas dissipated, and his discourse was heard afar until it totally faded. Jazmin had overcome the most terrible of fears.

That fear originated when people forgot gratitude and stopped looking at the beautiful side of life. She conquered over disapproval and pessimism, and most importantly, she did it confronting all these things with the love she expanded in the forest every time she breathed. Now, it was of vital importance that she keep herself within the high energies to easily flow towards The City of Pyramids, which was no more than the magical vision dwelling in the heart of an exquisite Crystal-Quartz.

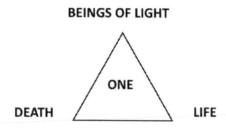

KING CICERO AND THE FOUR DRAGONS

Just a little ways beyond, four people were watching; they are the Guardsmen at the Temple gates; they were in charge of feeding the Mythical Dragons, who for eons were the Custodians of The Sacred Password. Ezequiel had told her so one night just before she went to sleep. A chilling sensation invaded Jazmin. Everyone was dressed up and their appearance was threatening. Their leader was a very large and robust man who looked like a barrel and had a weird crown. I stared at him and suddenly remembered him to be a king I'd seen in my childhood visions and dreams. The olden memory was really more from very far back; this king and I had known each other from a former life.

"I am Cicero The King; ruler of this city. You know, from here, I can manage the whole world, and especially those who never trust fate. Poor naïve little beings! They believe their future relies on their plans. They don't realize that they are no more than simple servants; idiots capable of running everything if we let them do what they want. These people, and all the people of The World, must be under my total control. Besides, I make lots of money doing it, so why not?"

I breathed and said, "Please, try to understand that not everything you've said is true. For hundreds of years, things have really changed. I suggest you start trusting."

"Silence! You wretched one!" he shouted. I saw him draw his sharp sword so, under such threatening circumstances, we chose to flee. Frightened, they were running as fast as they could across the field, while The King's soldiers were on their heels. Max suggested that we scatter out into separate ways and meet again later.

Jazmin arrived at the reflection of the temple in the middle of the field. A new dimension opened the way inside the image and she took a side corridor, all the while feeling someone stomping right behind her. She saw a door to her right, which happened to be ajar and went in, quickly closing it behind her and locking it as she could. She was right in the middle of The Central Pyramid's Virtual Hall. It was a huge room. She breathed deeply and could sense the smell of burning herbs. It was dark, and she sensed as if a bad omen was about to come. Her eyes were fixed on a spot about twelve feet above the floor; she was so terrified that she couldn't turn her back in time when she heard a very loud cracking sound.

Suddenly, a large furry beast snatched her and dragged through a corridor. She could barely take a wild guess at the dimensions of the huge monster that held her in between its claws. The devastating sight of what was before her eyes was about the most horrifying thing anyone could conceive of. The dragon was exactly the same as the one Ezequiel described in his stories of the woods. She knew these to be the images inside her mind. The fearsome dragon brutally let go of her, tossing her into a corner of that dungeon. Right then, Jazmin realized the monster was talking to her.

"What are you doing here, you foolish little woman? Did you lose something?", it would yell.

"You are so big, so very big," said Jazmin slowly.

"It seems you are in really big trouble," grouched the old dragon, custodian of that temple's east gate.

"Are you angry?", asked Jazmin.

"But of course! I have been here for tens of hundreds of years without being able to see sunlight. I just work and work and work to spook away all the princes and knights that have tried to pass through here; but they'll never succeed." It opened its ugly fetid big snout, and a big ball of fire came out, briefly lighting the dismal place.

Jazmin wanted to sit up, but her legs wouldn't respond. She was shaking out of the fear she felt before this horrifying presence and kept on talking from the floor in a soothing, kind tone.

"Perhaps you can talk King Cicero into giving you a vacation."

"That, I did a good many years ago. I remember it well. That's why they threw me away in the first place, in here and out from the woods. They thought I was a threatening monster that conspired against The

King. Then they condemned me to die of sorrow and confinement," it said visibly annoyed.

Jazmin gathered up all the courage left inside her and said: "So, you mean to say that you have never. . . left here?"

"Never," said the old dragon. "The King spared my life in exchange for me guarding this temple's east gate, but my eternal dream is to go out into the woods and fly freely. Deep inside, we dragons are really kind and would rather feed ourselves on flowers, although our outer appearance may terrify people. This is truly the first time somebody seems to be interested in what I feel. But what are you seeking in this temple?"

"Oh! Nothing special, I was just passing by and thought that just maybe, someone might want to talk a little."

"Bah! Go to another Dragon with that story! But now that I think of it, I'm starting to like you. You may come and talk to me anytime you so desire; after all, a foolish little woman like you represents no threat to the king's interests. I remember now, we dragons weren't always grumpy; when we lived out in the woods, we felt free and happy. It was the men, with their overwhelming authority, who lied and made everybody think we were boastful."

While the East Gate Dragon was talking (and rambling on about so many things he kept to himself for thousands of years and couldn't tell anyone through his endless solitude), Jazmin was listening carefully, breathing deeply, and slowly recalling events of happiness and peace. The surrounding heavy atmosphere was slowly changing, the room filling with a warm light and the dragon's behavior changing into fearlessness. He was slowly realizing that his anger was the key to his confinement and the destructive weapon of his great merits.

Light found its way back into being and The Dragon of The East started trusting again, remembering the beauty of the woods, and if just for one day, he chose to live it as if it were the last day of his life and without anger. And so, he was forever set free in a dream. Jazmin followed the ascending path within the temple until she arrived at the South Gate. She had a fixed stare towards nowhere in particular while thinking to herself: *Monsters are not always as bad as most everyone pictures them to be. Just think about how far down into darkness had this poor little giant come by believing in such nonsense.* She was facing The South Gate to the Temple and slowly pushed it in, trying to avoid any creaking sounds. Holding her breath simultaneously, she carefully went across the hall of entry hoping not to run into the Dragon keeping watch in the corridors.

She finally got to the main room of the temple's South wing, finding smoky ashes, a pile of burnt paper and a few pieces of burning coal (ember).

She knew for sure that the creature was lurking somewhere around the temple. Suddenly, a howling sound made her tremble in the shadowy-lighted place. She was continuously getting closer to finding The Sacred Password, which is crucial to the great transformation of humanity. Jazmin heard a very loud thump right behind her and one of earth's most terrible beasts appeared right behind her; it had the look of death and destruction in its eyes, moving just as serpents would and making this day look like one of the worst Jazmin ever had. It was right before sunset and time was running out to overcome this new situation.

There was something she knew: All of these monsters had a great need to express themselves to get rid of the chains that kept them tied to some secret.

"Ah. . ! I see a little woman who thinks she is going somewhere."

"Uhh. . . well, yes…" Jazmin admitted. "And you are…"

"Pleninumium, the most miserable of Dragons"

"Why do you say that?", Jazmin said.

"Because I take with me the Glory of everyone else's achievements. I live worried about everything; nothing is ever enough for me; money does not buy everything and is scarce and to my misfortune; there is always someone around asking me for things that I don't have. That is why I suffer and hate everybody. I can't stand for people to ask me for things. I just don't have them. I don't have them!" The seemingly desperate Dragon shouted. "Once I get rich and prosperous, I will set myself free and go far away from here. That is simple," said Jazmin.

"If all you want is to rid yourself from what you are presently lacking, all you have to do is to be more compassionate; give up all of what you have and all of what you are, with all your heart, so that all of your worries disappear out of your mind. In your mind, repeat your prosperity each day of your life in a constant reaffirmation so that it multiplies; you do this, and the universe will make sure that you get it back always."

"It is not so simple to live the way I live," The Dragon complained. "For thousands of years, my job has been to find people I could take valuable things from; that's the reason I am proud and convinced every step of the way that there really isn't enough for everyone; I know I'm right. Oh yeah… It has taken too much out of me; too much effort and too much struggle, Jazmin, and I'm tired of all this."

"Hmm… Let's see," Jazmin said. "What is the most wonderful thing about you? What would you do today if you were to have all the wealth of the universe at your disposal? How would you combine the thing you like the most about yourself and the thing you like to do best to help others in a compassionate way?"

The more this Dragon thought about all the possible answers to these questions, the more he changed the way he thought about himself, getting to the point of truly understanding the importance of giving, and realizing that giving is the basis and principle of receiving… but up to now, how much and what has he really given?

And from now on, what was he willing to give?

"May I suggest something to you?", Jazmin interrupted his thoughts. "Take me to the West Gate through the shortest path."

"And what will I get in exchange for doing that?"

"All the richness and prosperity in the universe forever."

"All right," said the Dragon. "I will take you there myself." Right when that huge being accepted to unconditionally give what at that moment was easiest to him (since he knew every inch to inch of the secret paths of the Temple), all around him was lit by a light, out of nowhere. He then discovered that all that time, he had been surrounded by the most incredible riches in gold, silver, and all kinds of jewelry, infinitely scattered all around the place, a luxury and comfort that had not unveiled before his eyes because during millennia, he was convinced that it was much too difficult to be prosperous. The Dragon finally realized that worry is the mother of poverty and that the compassionate giver has in store for him all the wealth, plentifulness and love.

Happily, he went through all the temple's paths and corridors, all the while celebrating his newly-found fortune and cheerfully singing thankful songs until they got to the West Gate right at dusk. And there it was: the angriest, most furious of all The Dragons. Even his brother feared it. Then,

Jazmin got up enough nerve and dared to ask: "What is wrong with you? Why are you so furious?"

The Dragon was swallowing its own fire, hurting its own bowels. It felt an extreme hatred towards itself and everything around it.

"I am worthless, a lost cause; nature was on vacation when I was born. I'm ugly and don't deserve anything other than suffering. Nevertheless, someone must pay for it. Perhaps if my mother had fallen in love with a rich, handsome Dragon, I'd be better off now," the Dragon complained. She asked: "Are you certain that you have taken a real good look at yourself in the mirror?" Out of nowhere, Plenilunium came up with a shiny silver cup where the reflection of his brother's countenance could be seen. In a very loving tone of voice, Jazmin said: "Take a look deep inside your eyes" … and so he did, for a few minutes, which seemed eternal. Meanwhile, Jazmin was breathing deeply, flooding the entire place with unconditional love and self-appreciation of her own inner beauty, a contagious energy which you only resort to in very extreme cases. Visibly moved, The Dragon had tears coming out of his eyes when he discovered his own inner beauty, recognizing his own majesty as one of nature's unique species, fortunate enough to be preserved with all his faculties and possibilities.

"So, I am the authority of my life. The King can no longer keep me chained to this confinement. I truly thank you Jazmin because within my eyes I could see my parents and recognize their grandeur as well as my own."

Jazmin was somewhat tired, but she had to close the cycle with happiness. The last door would leave free access to the center of the temple and there it was the motive of her search: The Sacred Password.

In an unusually bizarre way, all the spaces within the temple were lit, and outside, you could hear the footsteps of soldiers wanting to go into the virtual image. To no avail, since they were doing it out of utter fear to King Cicero's loud screaming who tirelessly repeatedly voiced:

"You shall not get through; I swear it, you will not get through!!!"

Jazmin could not turn back, now that she was so close to finding the fourth door; she just could not quit at this point. All of a sudden, she heard her own steps echo down below, underneath the floor, and she thought to herself: *The door has been simulated on the floor.* Hastily, she removed a large rug as she could, then opened a hidden little door, and a mouthful of fire welcomed her. Now she would have to enter and go through the basement of the temple; by now, she was wondering what would happen once she was down there. The high walls looked dark and full of mud; Jazmin could barely see amid the shadows a giant bent figure of slimy appearance. A deep-guttural voice said: "I see you've successfully convinced my brothers, but with me, it's a whole different story. It's not going to be so easy for you. I enjoy dishonesty and lies; I just love erring and taking away from others what they earn with their stupid integrity. What is it you are going to ask me? What would I want to do for others? Ha, Ha, Ha! Fine, I'll tell you... I want to keep on stealing from them all I can, the easy way or the hard way!", brutally screamed the dragon that didn't think he was worth anything at all.

"Hi!", Jazmin greeted him.

"What do you mean? Are you sleepy, or what?", replied The Dragon that by now was looking greenish under an odd, bright-foggy light, which made him look ghastly.

Right then, something struck Jazmin's mind and she understood that these Dragons were only memories that she had kept hidden away for over twenty years, and of which she had written about in one of her diaries. She remembered that once in her life, she wished to be a writer and for some time, she wrote about all her everyday worries since she felt confident and happy to trust that diary. She realized that The Dragon would get out of her way, totally transformed, as soon as she decided to think about all her achievements and all the things she had earned in her life through steady, honest-hard work. And once she recognized and fixed her total concentration on one of her highest strengths, namely, her authority, The Dragon would do that too. It would be enough to recognize the authority of her parents and teachers within her heart; and that is exactly what she did.

A gigantic door opened at one side of the temple and the marvelous nature of the woods manifested themselves before The Dragons. All their loved ones were waiting for them with a great celebration and they finally understood the great lesson which encompasses within the secret of the universe: they'd just discovered the gratitude and magic of choosing to see all the good.

Faltering to this principle affected Midas and King Cicero. They realized that they could have a new life-choice and that there was always a new opportunity for all those beings who choose to live each day of their lives under these principles: Don't let anything upset your peace. Always give love, out of your heart, to everyone. Honor your parents, your teachers, and yourself. Earn your work in an honest way and be grateful every instant of your life.

The Gates of Fear disappeared, and Jazmin knew that she had arrived at The Temple's Nave, the central hall, where right in the middle, an enormously giant golden sphere was floating, containing a crystal-like pyramid in its midst. there seemed to be Stemming from this pyramid, there seemed to be a very weird and wonderful symbol. Once again, she was vibrating in the world of dreams, and the warmth of the first rays of the sun invited her to continue with this great adventure. Her intuition wasn't fooling her. The moment had come for a new world to be born.

PART SIX

MEMORIES FROM THE FUTURE

THE CITY OF PYRAMIDS

The key to triumphing over The Dragons that guarded the Four Sacred Gates Jazmin went through, and to getting to the temple's main hall, was having kept herself connected to her feelings of love in her dreams. From the beginning of time, each one of the gates was guarded by fantastic beings born out of the essence of doubt. To fully comprehend the extent of the message, it was required for Jazmin to be watchful of her dreams, and above all, her own intuition.

By now, Jazmin consciously knew how to develop the energy: by concentrating on the beauty, forms, colors, and breathing and experimenting all the sensations, the flow of energy that goes back and forth through nature.

Jazmin had proven that The City of Pyramids was in the midst of an immeasurable Crystal-quartz. The Temple was on this magnificent pyramid's highest spot, which could be reached by going upwards in a counter-clockwise motion through a spiral-like trail surrounding the sacred mountain. She found out about this extraordinary city from the time she was a little girl through Ezequiel's stories and through the visions she often experienced in her dreams. She was convinced she knew every nook of the outstanding city just as well as she knew her grandpa's house and the cove. She closed her eyes, experiencing the magic presence of that portentous city that produced very intense sensations in her body. Jazmin was born into a new world at that precise moment, and the reunion with Ezequiel was imminent. It was necessary to increase the energy level within herself to a maximum in order to be able to observe the surrounding beauty and evoke the fountain of love within her heart, expanding it to an increasingly bigger, more intense sensation. Gradually, all the colors turned livelier and Jazmin could concentrate deeply on the blocking energy.

"It really hurts," she asserted.

"That is all right; breathe deeply and concentrate with all your strength on the exact spot where it hurts," Mr. Way said. "Inhale and aim a light-beam, saturated with unconditional love, where you are experiencing the pain; exhale and let the breath dissipate the pain into the cosmos."

Jazmin started to experience a strange tingling sensation while she listened and breathed. The pain started fading away. That is how pain lets you know where to place your attention for you to send energy of love and light to the cells so that atoms increase their vibrational rate to a higher one that purifies them, spreading a balanced health throughout the whole body. Now with a lighter, more energized body, Jazmin made her arrival into a hot and cloudy day, just like the day when she was born for the first time. She looked at the light breeze that made the treetops swing gently and the field looked as it were dyed with a golden light.

Unexpectedly, there were trees sprouting and growing to full length. The naturally spontaneous music usually heard in the woods was more intense, and that's when she thought about Ezequiel. She tried making the image of Ezequiel's memory sharper. It was like watching a video. Her heart was increasingly being filled by that special tingling and when least expected, an image of Max, Crosstemps, Urano, Mr. Way, Dominique, and herself, all walking together, side by side, came out. They all seemed to be surrounded by a brilliant blue light. All of a sudden, the entire moving luminescence came to a halt, since there, right by their side, was her Grandpa Ezequiel. "Thank God, my Grandpa is back!", Jazmin exclaimed with the greatest of joys.

Ezequiel had gone up so high that she could not find him from the earthly dimension, in spite of him being always by her side.

"What happened?", she asked. "Why is the music in the woods so loud? Where are we now?"

"This is a very special side to reality. It is here where dreams occur. Welcome to The City of Pyramids."

Right before her, there it was, emerging from the very womb of eternity: the majesty of that noble city, which for eons of millennia was petrified in the middle of a humongous crystal-quartz.

"Have you ever been here before?", Jazmin questioned Ezequiel.

"Many times, and none, really," he replied.

"Grandpa, so many things have occurred to me to get here and find you... I wonder... Did you succeed in finding The Sacred Password and meeting The Man that will change The World?", I asked.

"The truth is that we are still on our way."

With excitement, Jazmin started to vividly describe all that had occurred to her whenever she allowed fear to express itself. She had understood that danger is a phenomenon that occurs when people start believing in their pessimistic projections when they fear them as if they were happening.

"I believe I am here to get The Sacred Password and bring a new kind of Justice to The World, one based on true love. God is Divine Energy whose existence can be traced back way beyond rituals, sacrifices and public prayers. This is an internal psychological change based on a new type of nourishment to the ego with the fruit of knowledge."

"I am glad to hear that," Ezequiel said, visibly moved. "It means that my mission is partially accomplished, since the one called to find The Man that will Change The World is you Jazmin."

"Are you sure about that?"

"Absolutely! Right before you, a new era is unfolding, where State and Nation will, in a joint quest, work to promote a new kind of leadership, a new human civilization, and that happens to be the rebirth of The New Little San Juan."

Now she felt she could be truthful. Her intent and purpose fixed on the materialization of her dreams made the long-awaited miracle happen. She opened the eyes of the heart to appreciate the majesty of The City of Pyramids.

QUEEN REBECA AND PRINCE ARTHUR

Jazmin remembered that when she was in the middle of that enormous room, right by the sphere of light and The Sacred Password, a woman and a young man were interpreting strange music on the piano. They were facing her.

"Are they real? Or, is this a figment of my imagination?", I asked myself.

"I know you," the woman said in a very low tone of voice. "I am Rebeca, the Queen of The City of Pyramids." I looked at her for a moment filled with confusion. Her image was somewhat familiar to me. She had gone to Court to plead on behalf of her daughter, who had suffered several episodes of street aggression. She had finally rejected any attempt to relieve her grief, giving way to her lowest instincts. This daughter was just like her father.

"All is illusion," The Queen told me, with unusual kindness, while her son Arthur stopped playing the piano and turned his head my way. "Jazmin, please come with me," he whispered. Then, I remembered my friends and my Grandpa.

"What has happened to Grandpa and my friends? How come do you know my name?", I questioned.

"They are just fine; now, it is your turn to live the rest of the adventure. It is your time."

I turned my head to look for another door. *All of this is just inside my imagination*, I thought. How did you get to be here?

The woman took me by the arm and told me: "It has taken you hundreds of years to find a group like this. Are you going to run away once again? You have already experienced all the energy there is." The Queen's eyes were transformed into two balls of fire and I woke up in fear.

"Are you, all right?", Ezequiel asked as he hugged me. His facial expression evidenced a great relief.

"That was a strong dream," I told him. "And you put me directly into it."

"You slept for too long a time. The only thing we could do was to send you energy through our hands, our eyes, and our breath."

"Who sent all that energy?"

"The energy was sent by all of the souls who dwell in The City of Pyramids." When I looked, I saw thousands of beings making up an ascending, gigantic spiral, generating large waves of energy going through to the outer world.

"What is this place?", I asked my Grandpa, who was a wise man.

"The City of Pyramids is a construction of the mind of The Universe. In there, The Queen and her son, 'Arthur the righteous one', were witnesses to all that was occurring. The City of Pyramids is an ascending spiral; all of its streets were made of light and millions of souls sang day and night. It is that subtle sound, which at night is felt and heard on the earth's surface giving away, a living account of the existence of the world."

"The City of Pyramids, like the earth, is evolving and its inhabitants are also looking for the great truths of life." She remembered a few words: "It is important that we talk," Prince Arthur had told her with special kindness through her dreams when he invited Jazmin to his kingdom.

Jazmin decided to walk the streets of The City of Pyramids. A symphonic ensemble of wonderful beings inhabited that seemingly endless space located between thought and feeling. All the roads in the city formed a spiral in which it was easy to let oneself roll forever to infinity. Only the intentions of the heart were enough to ascend or descend as you wanted. While she walked through The City of Pyramids, all heads were turning, and continuous whispering followed Jazmin everywhere she went.

As above so below: now she understood what that really meant. She was counting the hours to get to the Central Pyramid and meet with Prince Arthur and his Queen Mother Rebeca. Everything in her is Faith, kindness, and Unconditional Love. She had spent the first one hundred and fifty thousand years of her marriage trying to make her husband understand all of these manifestations without success, until now. The queen was glad to receive Jazmin, and happily welcomed her, since she had been a part of her heart for eons in time, and in spite of all the sorrow, they were still a part of a great creation. She was still the same, only that a part of her had grown and matured towards another dimension.

"How could you be the wife of someone like King Cicero?"

"It is a very long story. When we both met, we would spend long hours talking and looking into each other's eyes. He used to tell me about all the wishes in his mind. He told me: 'I want to be a warlock, an international speaker. I'd like to leave an unforgettable print; be famous, be triumphant, and overcome many things. I want to have a house, happiness, a job that I like. I'd also like to be prosperous with prestige and have a close family who loves me and be honest with me. I want to have my own identity.' I could hear behind those words the true desire within Cicero's soul, a gentle voice that said: 'I, Cicero, want to find the real being within myself and reach a profound spiritual level. I want to work with God side by side, go through the right way of becoming a true master, and working myself through to the light by finding God.'

"I fell in love with that marvelous being, because deep inside, he wants to live peacefully, helping others to heal; he is a happy, tender, and kind being. A being who has eliminated out of his life all the revenge, anger, resentment, and prejudices. It was the promise of traveling, experience, trust, gratefulness, honesty, consciousness, respect, happiness, prosperity, to see and feel a close family; to be loved, which made me want to be next to this person. Cicero is the promise of illusion and another vision. Deep inside, he loves to dream, sleep deeply, hug dad, write a book, work create, handling himself well with others be restful...

But he does not seem to be that way. Once I started talking to him, he unsheathed his sword.

"It is just that Cicero has not yet understood that The Children of Creation have started to come out, one by one, loaded with mountains of forgiveness, peace and equilibrium. This fills him with pride because the innate qualities of these gifts radiate majesty, so Cicero's ego feels threatened and he attacks because he is trapped into one of fear's usual responses. You happen to be one of those beings, one of those children within the experience to be reborn, experiencing your own realization. You are endowed with the wonderful power of the self, capable of tolerance and forgiveness.

"The miracle has already started and all the birds in that world were flying, filled with happiness. The birth of a New World had begun. A very special atmosphere of transmutation flooded every space, while Queen Rebeca continued with her story. She tells us that to get to the point of evolution, you must go through a program of seven steps."

"If there is a method to get to this level, everyone who so wishes has a possibility to get there. But what would people do with all that knowledge?"

"They would have the opportunity to live in a healthy and stable body, with a sound mind and the ability to see the real truth in there. All of your emotions will be balanced to be happy you'd increase your level of vibration when you so wished and see The Father. You will be able to give more power to your work and accomplish your mission. You will be able to stabilize and harmonize your family because it is the source of your power. You will be able to build a better universe, one that goes back to the ways of unconditional love in everyone and everything."

"That sounds long and difficult. It is very costly, isn't it? How much do I have to invest?"

"Word at one-hundred-percent, it is worth letting go of fear so that you are able to give one-hundred-percent of your own spontaneity and capacity for improvisation. You must learn to lower your tone of voice to obtain one-hundred-percent of empathy, and for that, you have one-hundred-percent of courage."

PART SEVEN

GLOBAL

TRANSMUTATION

The Initiation

Jazmin observed that The Queen's necklace had two amethysts, a tourmaline, several pink and blue crystal-quartzes, and a golden pyramid with a strange symbol that seemed to float in the center of it. She had seen this same symbol in her dreams.

The Queen understood that the time had come for her to disclose the secret. She took off the necklace and placed it on Jazmin's neck. Immediately, thirteen smiling persons surrounded Jazmin, dancing joyfully around her with their hands raised towards the sky. A beautiful melody, born in the crib of universal love, awakened the feeling of unconditional love within their hearts. All of them liberated their tensions and fears in less than fifteen minutes. All of them understood that that special kind of energy (which healed the body and soul, unites a family, overcomes all blockages, comforts the spirit, loves the universe, and dwells in their hearts), is activated by integrity, trust, and love.

All thirteen persons approached Jazmin, one by one, to give her a sphere of light and color. The bright shades arranged themselves as a spiral turning from right to left and making up a beautiful rainbow. Jazmin started to visualize wonderful places in the universe being restored; forests, deserts, extinct animals, and all the people surrounding her seemed to communicate telepathically with her, sending her additional mental projections of places being restored in the world: jungles, deserts, extinct animals.

All the men surrounding her seemed to communicate telepathically with her and projected more restored places in the world. The knowledge of these men came from their hearts and penetrated everyone's. The universal

101

consciousness was expanding progressively, as all the men shared and expanded their wisdom from one heart to another. A large chrysalis of white light appeared over the heads of the men who were around Jazmin.

They were spheres of infinite light, a gift from heaven for health peace, tranquility, and material as well as spiritual development. The symbol in the middle of the pyramid was embedded within Jazmin. Curiously, she felt as if she was remembering and that had occurred to her in another time and place, a time when God had called for her to accomplish Gods mission. The mission is about the total transformation of man into the most sublime, creative-positive being on the face of The Earth. Now, she fully understood the extent of her sacred mission, since now she knows that she was called to be the guide for the Apostles of Light to come back.

REVELATIONS

The embedding of the sacred symbol marked the beginning of a series of experiences beyond logical explanation. All of the dreams transformed themselves into revelations of an unsuspected world. A thundering voice burst into Jazmin's internal peace, announcing eternal truths that forever were floating within time.

"The world is a pyramid of light," the thundering voice said. "The whole universe is based on three vertices. God is three energetic beings: the male energy, the female energy, and the universal energy; when these are mixed together, they form a sublime dynamical moving force. God's energy is equivalent to the square of the three vertices. The first vertex is made out of Gold and represents prosperity. The second vertex is made out of silver and encompasses all the energy of the beings that inhabit the physical world. The third vertex is made out of bronze, being in itself the threshold of transcendence between life and death." Jazmin was listening, paying special attention to what was said.

"This is the alchemical truth very well known in Atlantis. The Gold of truth permits the transfiguration of all the energy within gold, and at the same time, of gold within light. You are the light, that is the reason you will know the exact time when the light of men must be transformed into the gold of God's prosperity. Thousands of people will follow the message of God. Keep in mind that God is who really executes, and you are always his instrument. Alchemy is the basis of your life and your mission. It is the most powerful tool the world will ever know, because it will change man in seconds, with just one phrase, a touch of the hand, or a simple look. Peace is with you now and always blesses you in heaven and earth. The moment has come for your personal healing through love."

Four damsels came out of the four sides of the hall and washed with essences of cayenne, rose, jasmine, love, and prosperity. The sacred oil was placed behind her ears and on her back. The general atmosphere was one of peace, calmness, and material as well as spiritual development perfect to connect with The Creator. Jazmin was in complete ecstasy, letting her be taken by the blissful energy of the revelations. The Soccer Game was about to start.

THE SOCCER GAME

The weather was warm, and the nearby mountains looked especially green. It was Saturday and Samael will run his first official game after two thousand years of training. The game was between King Cicero's team "The Henchmen," and Queen Rebeca's team, "The Unicorns." Curiously, both soccer teams were formed by the nice inhabitants of the woods of Little San. All of them integrated man's most precious gifts and each one of them expressed human being's most sublime side. Mateo is a horse; Miguel is a kangaroo; Ricardo is a koala bear; Ruben is a handsome Saint Bernard dog; and Roberto, the goalkeeper, is a crab.

The perverse side of humanity was also expressed in The King's team. Federico is a bear; Jacinto is a rat; Tomas is a serpent; Atanasio is an eagle; and Francisco is a zebra. They, the inhabitants of the woods, along with all their sublime values and perverse actions, all had within their hands, the power to tip the scale, either way. If Rebeca's team won, she would become The Governess of The City of Pyramids for the next two thousand years. The news that Jazmin would be present in the game had leaked somehow, and this constituted very special luck to the Queen's team. Somehow, it was a good omen that the initiated one was there to support them.

The people of The City of Pyramids were willing to make sure that integrity and honesty were the guidelines of the competition. Those citizens wished from deep within their hearts for all things to flow in a normal way. They had decided that it was good for them to live in peace, in harmony, wealth and health. There was an ongoing rumor that, "The Henchmen", had developed at least seven hundred thousand and one ways to cheat; among which, many simulated accidents may be pointed out. These so-called "accidents" could cause the death of the players, and even the sudden disappearance of the honest referees.

All of the inhabitants in The City of Pyramids had concentrated their energies in the success of their team, because it was the guarantee of their liberation, the real possibility of starting a new life, and transmuting to The City of Pyramids in the promised land that is. Meanwhile, King Cicero's team was looking for even more ways to tip the balance in their favor.

By eleven o'clock in the morning, the Grand Central Stadium, located next to the Central Pyramid, was filled up with spectators. Both teams were getting ready in the dressing rooms. King Cicero's acolytes were dressed up in black and white clothes; and those faithful to The Queen were dressed in green and white. The players stepped on the soccer field in the middle of great cheering and applause. Up from the rows, fans of both teams were crying hurrahs aloud.

Jazmin was seated right beside Queen Rebeca in the royal box. She remembered that soccer had always been her grandpa's favorite game. Ezequiel's wise words also came to mind: "A soccer referee looks for the coincidences, virtues, and linking points between the confronting parts. Confrontation is the essence of unity, since there lies the origin of dialogue, communication, understanding and learning of all human beings. The dialogue occurs by two people having communication maps, in order to be able to see, through God's dynamical energy, the solutions to any given situation. The bridge is achieved with the intelligence and with the wisdom of giving everyone what is fair and what corresponds to them as long as it is done with truth and equilibrium, where everything flows in unity.

"Life is like a football game, where it does not matter who wins, but to give the best effort with love and give the spectators the best possible performance that they deserve. The spectators must be educated with firmness, steadiness, subtlety, and love. A love from the leadership, the example, the integrity, the unity of the being, the recognition of its essence, of its virtues, of its own personal, family, labor and social leadership. The public is everyone, the referee is the one, and the one is God. The bridge of communication and dialogue is God; that is, unity, which is achieved when the potentials of human beings emerge. Potentials such as charisma, rectitude, and intelligence. Intelligence is understood as the analysis of the situations of life, the internal vision and practice of wisdom, where the lived experiences of each person are obtained without prejudice, without complexes, without grudges. Charisma is a gift. Rectitude is the essence."

The time for truth had arrived at The City of Pyramids, and that feeling, like the aroma of success, was breathed throughout the city. The hour, so long awaited by the inhabitants of The City of Pyramids, had finally arrived. This was the day when all of their illusions, hopes, and wishes for change could come true, and it all depended on the interrelationship between two important factors: Positive energies and a clean game. This meant the transformation of the aspirations of the people to be able to get a government centered in values such as Justice, Truth, Common Good, and Respect for their Rights. In The City of Pyramids, people would like to feel that their participation is important and recognized; that their ideas are the fundamental pillar for the construction of the new society they all deserve. The stridency of a trumpet silenced all the spectators concentrated in the Central Stadium. A thick, loud voice filled the atmosphere; it was the sports commentator of the broadcasting channel, "The Voice", who announced: "Ladies and gentlemen, welcome once again to The Central Stadium of The City of Pyramids. The moment of truth has arrived. We have all been waiting for this very day, where our destiny is at stake. We are here to witness The Game of The Millennium between King Cicero's official team, 'The Henchmen,' versus Queen Rebeca's team, 'The Unicorns.'" A large number of fans spread throughout the rows were offering hurrahs and applauses to King Cicero's black and white reckless team.

The teams were ready to jump in the soccer field. They were just a few minutes away from the start of the game. The busy coaches gave instructions to their players. Curiously, there was just a small group of people supporting Queen Rebeca's team, "the Unicorns." A roaring shouting came from out of the rows. Booing, hooting, and insults on the part of The Henchmen's fans were aimed at Queen Rebeca's team, followed by hurrahs and applauses for King Cicero's team when they came out into the field. Their coach, General Midas, guided "The Henchmen;" they wore white sweatshirts with a black collar and an emblem in the center of the chest with King Cicero's face in the middle of it.

First came Federico, whose alias was "Bear", one of the most famous goalkeepers of the league who was famous for his good playing, conceited personality, and superiority complex, which more often than not, created ill-conduct towards others. There was also Jacinto, the team's star forward.

He was also known for showing off falsehood and cunning, a skillfully negative subject. Tomas was a strong forward, valuable to King Cicero's team for his dirty game. Atanasio showed up haughty and arrogant; yesterday, he made a statement to the press: "I already feel sorry for Queen Rebeca's team; it is a shame, since it is a mediocre non-effective team." Wearing black and white stripes painted on his face, Francisco was considered the strongest defender "The Henchmen" had; his motto was: "Pass the ball, not the player." "The Henchmen" were on the referee's left-hand side; they emphasized their gestures of rage with hard faces and the feeling that they would win, no matter what means they used to do so.

Samael, who was the coach to Queen Rebeca's team, contemplated the scene, and in his heart, vibrated the hope that they would win playing a clean game. The luminous whiteness of the sweatshirts of his team contrasted with their green collars. This was a team of dreamers: "The Unicorns".

Mateo, the team's captain, was a proud exponent of nobility and ethics without equal. His game could only be executed with integrity and cleanliness. Next to him was Miguel, a fast, quick, clean, and effective player. Ricardo was good for opening spaces, famous for being a good dribbler, and due to his mobility and genius, constituted a key player for quick comebacks to his team.

Ruben was a helpful defender, honest, a great friend, and a teammate whose every play on the field was filled with passion and surrender. Lastly, we had Roberto, the goalkeeper, who stood out for his colorful uniform, stamped in olive-green and white. His ever-smiling lips, his good of humor, honesty, and professionalism were the keys to his having so many admirers.

All the conditions were given to start The Great Game that will define The City of Pyramids' fate for the next two thousand years. The bright goal lines had a special net made out of pure energy shaped in the form of an arch; these had already been checked out by the auxiliary referees.

The main referee held a luminescent soccer ball; it was an energetic sphere. He was now ready to start the game with his initial whistle-blow. He then called the captains to the center of the field, reminding them of some of the basic rules of the game:

"Remember that the ball can be touched with any part of the body, with the exception of the hands, arms, and forearms. You may make telepathic throws with the mind by sheer concentration. The ball may be hit in the air. Fouls such as tripping, hard blows, pushing, stepping on each other, etc., will be sanctioned. In the case of any advanced position of any of the players, the play will be invalidated, and it will be regarded as an indirect shot at the goal line in favor of the other team."

Samael told his boys:

"All right my friends, the time for the truth has arrived. God blesses you right now. As always, I want an honest, clean game, where compassion will lead us to the miracle of a victory."

Everyone in the stadium, players and spectators alike, stood up as a sign of respect to listen to the notes of The Universal Anthem. It is a moment of faith where some make the sign of the cross over themselves or make sacred reverences to protect themselves by invoking the sacred presence and guiding fate through the assistance of divinity. The referee signaled the goalkeepers, and they nodded their heads as a sign that everything was ready to start the game.

A long, loud whistle-blow was heard, and the luminescent sphere was floating in the middle of the field. The game had started, and "The Henchmen" had the ball. Jacinto quickly passed the ball to Francisco, who immediately passed it to Tomas, running on the left flank and opening his space through by kicking, tripping, and pushing Mateo, making his way swiftly to his opponent's goal line.

The coach of "The Unicorns", Samael, shouted from the bench, "Referee, foul!", to no avail, since this referee was not paying attention to any complaints. At that moment, Tomas received the ball and shot it in the air, making a medium height, half-moon-like course in the direction of the opposing frame; running very rapidly, Jacinto and Ruben dove towards the flying ball. Jacinto got to hit the ball first with his fist, changing its course to the lower right side of the goal line, making Roberto's dive to stop the goal useless. Right then, Mateo and Ruben protested, but to everyone's surprise, the referee pointed to the center of the field, indicating that the goal was valid.

Protest came and went among the spectators and "The Unicorns" team players. Indignation took hold of most everyone present. Mateo, taking control of the situation, addressed his teammates: "Take it easy! We are a great team. The truth is light, and it is with us; let's go!"

The team's favorable reaction changed its whole attitude. The faces of the players lit up, evoking a potent flow of motivation running within. Thus, Ricardo touched the ball, passing it to Miguel, and he passed it to Mateo, who galloping his way through, dribbled to Atanasio and then to Francisco, immediately kicking deeply the ball to Miguel, who in turn, ran diagonally to the left, leaving Federico behind and inside the big area. When he was ready to score, back, from behind, Francisco made a sweeping slip, tripping Miguel to the ground. Mateo, Roberto, and everyone else on the rows, shouted in unison: "Penalty!"

Surprisingly, the referee indicated for the game to go on and signaled to take a goal kick. The whistling and booing towards the central referee from the audience was deafening and in the midst of the protest, the loud voice of General Midas could be heard cheering his players and saying: "Well done, Francisco! Now they know who's the boss!". Once again, the spectators whistled and booed, but this time in protest to General Midas' attitude. All the while, the people as a sign of disagreement and disapproval, waved white handkerchiefs protesting about the demeanor of "The Henchmen."

The following minute transpired in between exiting plays on the part of "The Unicorns" and with more of the same brutal plays on the part of "The Henchmen," where kicking, pushing, sweeping, etc., prevailed, before the cynical stare of the referee, who without exception would allow for such actions contrary to all game rules. Suddenly, the whistle was heard, and the first half of the game was over.

This was the opportunity for both coaches to review their strategies and give further instructions to their respective players.

Meanwhile, in this intermediate time, all the people were booing the infuriated King Cicero, who uttered out these words: "You, ungrateful, traitors, conspirers!" At that point, Jazmin, who was seated to the right of Queen Rebeca in the Royal-box, stood up and looking straight to The King with the truth in her eyes, in a compassionate way, told him in a warm voice: "You are only reaping what you have sown." The King turned his head and ignored her.

At this time, "The Unicorns" team players came out, and a thundering sound of applauses, hurrahs, and singing erupted, definitely evidencing the preference of the onlookers.

Everything had changed in a matter of minutes, since by now, the public was aware of the reigning dishonesty. Next thing, "The Henchmen" came out with a clear-cut protest among the fans.

Jazmin and Rebeca looked at each other. Without the mediation of any words, they both understood that the time had come to interconnect all the consciousness of the spectators to the energies of Love, Justice, Truth, Honesty, and Common Good. A halo of white light started to project from out of Rebeca and Jazmin, creating a sublime, spiritual, and real connection with all the people assisting to the game. The worn-out followers of "The Henchmen" started crying copiously, while the rest of the people knew in their hearts that The Power of Justice, Truth, and Love was inside them and that was all the strength they needed to prevent and stop injustice and unbalance in the game.

For some unknown reason, the energy that Jazmin was breathing in and out connected everyone in The Grand Stadium, and very soon, tenseness took hold of the entire scene.

The City's Natural Leaders had gathered up in common accord, just in case King Cicero and his team, coached by General Midas, once again tried to change the rules or attempt to hurt in any way the referees.

Very soon, one of the King's players had closed the way of Queen Rebeca's star player, hitting him hard.

"Foul!" The fans of the green and white team shouted. The uproar made everyone think something other than the tribunes would fall down if those kinds of actions continued.

"Referee, what happened to the red card?" Ezequiel was screaming from the tribunes. The referee was having a hard time being impartial.

Right after such evident cheating, the revolt started. In a few minutes, all was in great confusion; collective fear that dishonesty and trickery might win the game generated great tension among the onlookers that almost degenerated into mass-hysteria. Up to this point, anything could happen. Jazmin was really having a hard time keeping herself focused on The Breath of Love.

All of a sudden, everyone around was turning his or her attention to Jazmin. Within herself, she had the power to transform that entire reckless scenario into harmony. Conflict and fear of losing because of a people's revolt were reflected in the soccer game. Right then and there, Jazmin understood what it was that she was trained for all this time. She had recognized within herself the living essence of The Man Who Changes the World, whose mission is to give back to others the vision of their true selves as being equally powerful.

"Come on Jazmin," desperately whispered Queen Rebeca and Prince Arthur.

She centered her attention on her breath, clasping her hands above her heart. Thick-blue flames started coming out of her body, surrounding her, and turning into a giant hurricane of blue light, expanding itself throughout the whole place and beyond, until it covered the entire City. The miracle of the game gave way to a new energy of change within all the beings in The City of Pyramids, and The Woods of Little San Juan. The girl started to do her job. All the inhabitants of The City of Pyramids realized that they had the power within themselves to change everything around their lives.

The whistle sounded again to indicate that the second half of the game had started. The willingness of "The Unicorns" was clear enough. Now was the time to win and fuse the victory to the feeling of change and transformation, which all the citizens of The City of Pyramids claimed.

Miguel kicked the ball off. He passed it onto Ricardo, who sent it to Ruben. Ruben who was running by the right side, took the ball and extended his path up to the final line, marked by Francisco, producing an airborne center, to the point of penalty where Miguel gave it a head-shot into the right upper quadrant before an unbelieving Federico, who was impotent to do anything about it. He held his head with both of his hands because of the goal that evened up the actions.

The crowd was overwhelmed with emotion jumping up and shouting, "Goal! ... Goal! ... Goal!"

"This is a great day for 'The Unicorns," the sports commentator pointed out. "It is the day that we will be free, and everyone will win!" The ball was returned to the center of the field, and "The Henchmen" felt annoyed and impotent because their tricky dirty game wasn't going to work anymore for them.

Mateo signaled his teammates by saying: "Synchronization!", and the players, just like lightning-bolts turned into virtual light-beams, kept their silhouettes and linked up in telepathic communion. Samael informed the others that there was just one minute left. Without warning, all the fans stood up and in unison started repeating in a chorus-like voice: "Unicorns, Unicorns, "Unicorns!". Jazmin, Rebeca and Arthur stood up too, achieving the required spiritual connection.

A strike of luck in the form of a spiral of energy surrounded all the Grand Central Stadium. All the spectators, the players, and the field as well, were enclosed within this energy, while King Cicero, Midas and, "The Henchmen" watched in awe without understanding what was happening.

It was "The Henchmen's" kick-off and Tomas passed it to Jacinto, who combined with Atanasio, who flew the ball through the right side, hoping not to be intercepted. In that precise instant, out of nowhere, Mateo and Ruben were awarded a pair of golden wings each, intercepting Atanasio by fair means. They took the ball of light from him and Mateo recovered it.

Up on the rows, everybody was watching with their mouths wide open due to how the game scenario had risen up from the ground. Now the game was being played on the air. Mateo, through a telepathic command, passed the ball to Ricardo, who up from the air, sent the ball into a deep pass on the left side, where Miguel received it. Being marked by Francisco and Tomas, he feinted the first one, and then the second one, taking the ball in front of the goal line and facing Federico, who came out to meet him. Intelligently, Miguel brought the ball down to ground level and kicked the ball just above Federico's head, tracing a rainbow-like flight of light and placing the ball inside the goal line and into the net, before the confused looks of Federico, Midas, Cicero, and the astounded players of "The Henchmen" team. The people were kicking up a tremendous row all throughout the stadium. The magic of the energy of light and bliss took over The Grand Central Stadium, making this contagious feeling spread throughout the city as well. Within seconds, the news spread out like gunpowder. "The Henchmen" were ninety seconds from losing this game, bringing along with this devastating defeat, the surrender of power for the next two thousand years. An atmosphere of joy, festivity, illusion, and faith was evidenced. There was another kind of reality because the hands of all the citizens were already caressing the new change.

The next few seconds passed by between the increasingly desperate efforts for Jacinto and Tomas to score, and the fairness and solvent equilibrium of "The Unicorns."

At last, the golden moment Queen Rebeca and the people of The City of Pyramids had longed for during many years had finally materialized.

The referee's whistle blew, indicating the end of the game. The triumph of the truth, principles, and values that oriented the life of the citizens of The City of Pyramids had materialized. Perhaps Midas would never know what had happened. The King could not stop crying, cursing the members of his team. Within the next few days, it would be known what the position of King Cicero was, who in his initial statements, stated the game was a fraud.

He affirmed that he would not leave power under the compassionate gaze of Jazmin, Rebeca, and Arturo, who aimed their energetic connection of good intentions to the king.

Little by little, in between tears, the plump figure of the king was stylized, his skin was getting paler, and the transformation was in progress. The events of the day seemed to have changed the ideas that King Cicero had until today about life.

A part of his thought tried to rebel against the changes and at some point, he thought that he was falling victim to some strange hex. But his heart did not deceive him; within himself, the truth exploded, and he felt enraged with himself for having allowed fear to govern his city and his wonderful people. Repentance was touching the King's heart.

That day the simple people of the City of the Pyramids understood, as did many nations of the world that had maintained the tragic lie of a false peace for two thousand years. That the key was found simply by following the dictates of the heart.

Jasmine infinitely thanked the wonder and beauty of that world and the unforgettable experience of living in truth. She understood the importance of having a north of love and power, because all the inhabitants of this and other worlds were worthy of all success and happiness.

The peace in her heart was the key to the peace of the world. Good deeds and bad deeds are two sides of the same coin and the eternally lasting is the one.

Jasmine suggested that this teaching had to be available to all as a constitutional right, as it constitutes the life force: to lift the world from the destructive domination of fear. Then King Cicero, committed to his

Queen Rebekah, yielded power to his son Arthur who said: "If my life reaches to encourage this teaching, my death will not be in vain."

Never before had Jazmin been so calm. She felt an overwhelming peace that was telling her that everything was always fine in spite of the outer appearances.

PART EIGHT

A RE-EVALUATION OF THE ADVENTURE

NEW MISSION, NEW LAW

Jazmin had come back from a fresh, new world, like just having been born. She was in the middle of the spring of the world. She only breathed and wrote down whatever the voice of her heart told her, and her notes defined a new mission and a new law.

"Fairness is always within our hearts." Backing up this premise, a new order was initiated in The City of Pyramids. Self-trust and trust in others would be the basis for the creation of progress and development in The City of Pyramids from now on. Consequently, the basis for wealth would not be measured by the money the people had, but by the degree of harmony, serenity, and peace they shared.

God's supreme energy was speaking through Jazmin and addressing all the citizens: "This world's governments will truly be successful when they teach their citizens to love, to respect, to work, to prosper, and to understand that money is just a circumstance that comes and goes, but if you do the right thing, it will never be scarce.

"Everyone will recognize the essence of success as the progressive realization of a dream. A dream is the overpowering desire to reach spiritual and material development. If people would convince themselves that, they can generate self-esteem, and a trust in their own potentials to get emotional mastery, they will be able to experience a sense of security, peace and spiritual tranquility."

The people of The City of Pyramids came to accept that steady work with love, constant trust, and honesty generate self-esteem and made them productive. Now, they easily understood that leadership required that individuals know themselves and others. Working communities should learn a new managerial system, with individuals and their families, based on a solid foundation of three main pillars of communication, love, and respect. This may be in tune with their true life-mission, integrating themselves to their work group with enough planning to carry out important tasks to the social and entrepreneurial organizations.

Nature looked especially beautiful. It was easy to be aware and accept society as a living organism with a life of respect, self-compromise, and a conscientious sensitivity to community matters. From now on, life would be considered and organized as a horizontal structure where the kind of society that everyone wished for, to live and experience, could be achieved in The City of Pyramids.

The State is the instrument through which all human societies would develop, as long as they did it with love, self-awareness, and an acknowledgment that The Father is within all human beings.

The virtue of communication is not in saying nice things about life, but in feeling, living, appreciating, and believing what you say and in being convinced one hundred percent of your word as being light, and that light is God and God does not err in what he says.

When you speak from intellect alone, ego, prejudice, and indifference are speaking; but when you speak from the heart, everything will be transformed. Communication is life and words have the power to drive emotion. When you are flowing with love, the sincere expression that makes your communication of love cheerful comes out.

To live is to be authentic and being authentic implies that you are one with and within God. To be one with God means to feel that a bird flying is freedom and freedom is like an eagle gliding in the sky. Wisdom is like penetrating thought. It is like appreciating everything we see. Ego is a castle of life where the king is you. You are a king who manages his own life by will alone, but who also lives in his kingdom knowing that a word has the power to change the world. Truth is to be able to see the entire picture, where you can see the energy of chaos as well as the energy of life; being both expressions of intelligent, dynamical and transmuting energies of the universe. Chaos is not the representation of physical death, but of spiritual death itself. On the other hand, Light is chaos elevated from its very essence to the highest levels of vibration. There are seven vibrations or levels:

Alpha	
Beta	TERRESTRIAL BEING
Gamma	
Ultra-Gamma	SPIRITUAL BEING
Luminum	
Platinum	STELLAR BEING

Plelulium

This is the highest level of essence of all. Just a few beings have attained this level. Of those you know, there are only three of them: Jesus, Buddha, and Gandhi; the others are from other galaxies.

To raise your vibration, you must be in tune with your inner peace, meditate, and program your life and the life of all around you in a positive way; it is about conceiving the world with compassion and tenderness and with the illusion of living and experiencing the most wonderful moment in your life.

Mercy: I am that representation. I am the vibration that picks up the rest of vibrations. The spiritual world is a wide universe and you are a part of it. Your new mission is:

— To live in peace with your fellow men.
— To live in peace within.
— To live in peace in your thoughts
— To live in peace with life.

Mercy is love. It is believing that everything is possible. It is forgiving with the heart. Forgiving is the absolute transformation of the energetic lie into an inner truth of the light. It is living feeling you may live and die in an instant. It is to understand that we all are one, that we are a team now and ever.

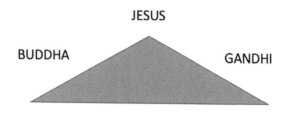

Giving is the sublime spring of love. Receiving is the pleasant experience of giving. Giving and receiving are one, and we are one now and ever. Prosperity goes through the knowledge of being one. It occurs when I, as a being of light, recognize the abundance in my heart, and enjoy the peace and abundance of the universe. Today, tomorrow, and forever, I am a son or daughter of the prosperity I recognize in myself. The light of life is the powerful spring of creation, where flowing and finding oneself are the same; that's why happiness in the human being is given to him (or her) by his heart and not by his reason.

Feel the peace within, as well as the love of God running through your body. Recognize yourself within and for the light, since infinity is within you today and always forever and ever. Life and death are a part of the same essence. Light, the illusion of living and dying, is simply that; just an illusion within true life, which transcends the halo of light that you are, because life is much more than just living. It is to transcend within the one, now, and ever through infinity. God has chosen us for this stage and we cannot fail, for you will do marvelous things in this incarnation. Start walking. You must start flowing and tell God's truth.

The light is the truth within Christ, The Man, and The God. Feel the presence of the living God within and the transformation will happen. For love did Christ die and for love will we triumph within him. I am that, now and ever. He who believes in me will be free, without any barriers or prejudices, since he can do all and can see all. I am the truth hidden within you. I am your truth and your salvation. Search for the truth, search for love, and look for the happiness of feeling yourself as the son of God and you will know what it is to be free. Hate and love are insufficient-incongruous bonding which help you grow once you set yourself free of them. Mastery of love is accomplished through the practice of breathing. Breathe to link up with the true essence of life and the universe.

Pure consciousness is universal consciousness as anyone could find it because it is within the self, which is an infinite-unlimited and loving being. God's limitless consciousness is within all of us. It is there when you cry or laugh. And with each step you take, is God's consciousness there.

Love, Faith, and Compassion are the pillars of divine consciousness, since love is the one energy that sets everything into motion and therefore is within anything and all: Faith is the unrestricted belief in the limitless-self within each one of us. Compassion is the understanding of the truth that we, human beings, are boundless light-beings living in a physical world. The truth of self is that we are love now and ever. I am truth and life, he who believes in me shall never die. A blue light-beam in the world gives protection to the universe. You only have to ask for protection; your light is my light; the truth of the world is love inside you today and always. Good and evil are a part of the same. A pure being will always be so, even if his dark side is present.

"You must understand that we are compromised to do our best, no matter what would be happening behind life-scenarios," said the voice of God.

"I seem to be seeing things more clearly," said Jazmin. "Being sorry for the past and afraid of the future are the twin webs fright uses to keep us bound to its insignificant demands and its wrongful advises."

"The set of techniques is being given to you now, for you to rise from the mental awkwardness generated by fear and will be called The Golden Alchemy."

"Golden Alchemy?", Jazmin asked.

"Yes, the one origin of all that exists. This is The Sacred Password, which allows humanity to live in a high-consciousness-state since the dawn of time, where God is ever present. It is the key to overcome the limits of a deceitful dimension and recognize ourselves as universal light-beings and truly co-creators with God.

Man's life is like an immense crystal-quartz, which dyes of many colors the shiny white of eternal truth.

The new law is:

I can see love within you.

I will never be anything more than what I am.

All that exists within me has been my own creation.

JOSÉ MANUEL RIZZO

I create life.
I create love.
I create death.
What you see is your projection in me.
Transmutation is the renewal of your mind.

PART NINE

THE RETURN HOME

A NEW HISTORY

Jazmin finally understood that her encounter with Ezequiel was God's gift to her, for her consciousness and spirit to accept that there was only one truth: the truth of love, compassion, and justice.

Jazmin had a vision in which the inhabitants of The New Little San Juan started adoring her and asking her for miracles. A large crowd surrounded her, asking her for magic and healing. Some of them asked that she change their lives with a small drop of water, or with a medal.

At that very moment, Jazmin knew that people needed something other than pure touch and feeling. She knew that God's energy had to go into their hearts for them to truly understand that the magic was inside them and within the same God we are a part of. Jazmin remembered that moment before the crowd and the cheers for having won the football game. She then, called upon the energy of the Father to come down to her and right away Mr. Way showed himself as she had never seen him before. He looked like a halo of light shaped like a silhouette with three incandescent light-beams, melting within each other, turning into one light beam. The beam was pointed directly and touched Jazmin's pyramid, the one she had pending on her chest.

Jazmin was experiencing illumination, and through her heart, she was connected to Queen Rebeca and Arthur, the new King of The City of Pyramids. That is how the light started to expand through all the inhabitants of The City of Pyramids as well as all the animals of the woods of Little San Juan, whom by feeling the light started to cry out of joy and happiness.

All those beings rediscovered themselves as a part of that energy. They discovered that they didn't need water, nor candles or incense, to be connected to The Father.

The energy started expanding in all directions and the entire town seemed to be floating up in the air. An immense rainbow covered the sky from The City of Pyramids to the New Little San Juan. Above the rainbow, Ezequiel appeared riding Crosstemps and with Dominique flying at his side and with the company of Max and Urano. It was a moment of sublime connection with the energy coming out of Mr. Way's hands as very intense beams of light.

The energy turned into a giant rug of Crystal and pink quartz. A rug that mixed purity and unconditional love. The rug extended, giving Jazmin the possibility to either stay and accomplish her mission in the New Little San Juan or proceed with the adventure beyond the threshold of reality. She knew it was the last time within this time, within this space that she would see her Grandpa, although they would find each other again in another adventure of time and space.

"Had I known before, that truth and love were always within me, my life would be another life," Jazmin said.

"Whatever comes out of your heart is what is important, since now you know that present, past and future don't matter anymore. Energy is much more than that and you are a part of that energy; the key to change anyone's life is within the heart of an innocent child," said the thundering voice she was in contact with since she entered the sacred temple.

"What will I do now?", Jazmin asked.

"Love is everything," said a choir of all her friends and Grandpa Ezequiel, who had decided to stay to continue with the adventure into higher planes. At that moment, Jazmin started to raise towards the sky, surrounded by The Angels of Air, Water, Heaven, and Fire, and. melting into the rainbow. She was on her way back to Little San Juan and everybody was waving goodbye. While still in the air, she was promising that she would go back to teach the way to others. The city was illuminated; it was raised to another level, and its inhabitants as never before, saw how all their negative emotions came out and where it was purified.

The time had come for her to choose between staying within the vision or going back to spread out the message: "Our destiny is to create love; whenever we increase love, fear evaporates dazzled by the perfect light".

Once again, the cosmic sound of the waterfall, like a storming voice, made everyone aware of the universal vibration. It was the molecules hitting each other inside The Godhead and singing in unison the generating mantra of a new tomorrow and a new history.

Jazmin took it upon herself what she had to assume. She hopped on her rug and while looking at Mr. Way, she said, "I know who you are! You are who you are. You are the one who will always be. God bless you and I thank you for being always at my side, guiding me into the light. God bless you Father for having transformed these people, and for loving me and everyone else."

For an instant, time came to a standstill. Space was one and one end of the rainbow put itself underneath the rug, and started to rise, leaving a streak of light behind her. The people of the new Little San Juan started to wave at her sending her their best thoughts and wishes. At the distance, a pink energy of love could be sensed, and the town's inhabitants came to understand that this was the beginning of a road to truth. It was the beginning of an adventure entrusted to them by their creator.

A large door of white light opened up in the sky and from there, Ezequiel was saying: "I know that you will always be with me, because you have always been, and my love towards you is and will always be an unconditional one."

Just then, Jazmin turned around and said:

"I bring a message of peace to all of you, a message of love and justice. I have come back to share with you everything I have lived, and to invite you to keep on going through the adventure of life under the direction and advise of our good friend Mr. Way."

That was the best return home in Jazmin's life; it was much better than looking at the sacred lights in the woods of Little San Juan. Never ever would she forget that instant in her life.

THE END

JOSÉ MANUEL RIZZO

He is a Doctor of Science in Alternative Medicine. A Life Coach and Health Coach. He has an Ms. in Mental Health and an Ms. in International Entrepreneurial Coaching and Mentoring. He is the Founder and CEO of Coninrec, CA and Global Sider CA. He is a Spiritual Master, with an emphasis on working with Archangels. He is a Japanese Reiki Master and Egyptian Reiki Master. Master training in Neurolinguistics Programing. Lawyer. Master  in International Rights of Human Rights, International Criminal Justice and International Humanitarian Rights. Specialist in Business Law and International Contracts. Former Professor at the Andres Bello Catholic University, Writer, Motivator and International Speaker. Author of the Programs and Certifications of Creative Reengineering and Reiki Golden Alchemy. His experience as a Lawyer started in 1991 and he has been a Doctor of Science in Alternative Medicine since 2007. Doctor Rizzo is permanently invited to TV shows to give useful advice in the health field with a holistic perspective.

His constant preoccupation toward man's growth and development has driven him to do research and go into an in-depth study of century-old disciplines such as Reiki-Ho for Natural Healing. Mastering these techniques at the Usui Reiki Gakkai in Japan, and the Spanish Reiki alliance, among other prestigious organizations.

Certified Teacher in Spiritual Response Therapy.

He is an author of Creative Reengineering Program.